## ROOM 13

The stairs took a turn and went on up. As Fliss climbed, it grew colder. There was another landing, more doors and another turn  third landing, then a fourth, more stairs. She was at the were four doors, each with a n As she read the numbers door thirteen swung inward with a squeal. 'No!' she whispered, but it was no use. Her feet carried her over the threshold and the voice hissed 'The Room of Doom.'

## INSIDE THE WORM

The worm danced sinuously through the darkening garage, its great head swaying and bobbing. Fliss was amazed at the dexterity of her friends. The way their dancing feet avoided the great train of fabric they trailed, which slid, hissing, across the dusty concrete. When she remembered to look at her watch it was ten to ten.

'Hey!' Their exultant laughter drowned her voice. 'Hey, you guys. It's almost ten. I've got to go.' Nobody heard.

'Lisa?' they mimicked, and her voice was among them.

'Lisa, Lisa, Lisa, Lisa –' the worm was coming at her now, eyes burning, jaws agape. She turned and fled...

# ROBERT SWINDELLS

## ROOM 13
### and INSIDE THE WORM

Illustrated by Jon Riley

CORGI

ROOM 13 and INSIDE THE WORM
Room 13 was inspired by a real school trip to Whitby by Year Two,
from Mandale Middle School in Bradford, 1987.

A CORGI BOOK 978 0 552 55591 3

ROOM 13
Doubleday edition published 1989
Corgi Yearling edition published 1990
Reissued 2000, 2007

INSIDE THE WORM
Doubleday edition published 1993
Corgi Yearling edition published 1994
Reissued 2000, 2007

1 3 5 7 9 10 8 6 4 2

Copyright © Robert Swindells,1989 and 1993
Illustrations copyright © Jon Riley, 1989 and 1993

Corgi Books are published by Random House Children's Books,
61–63 Uxbridge Road, London W5 5SA,
a division of The Random House Group Ltd,
in Australia by Random House Australia (Pty) Ltd,
20 Alfred Street, Milsons Point, Sydney, NSW 2061, Australia,
in New Zealand by Random House New Zealand Ltd,
18 Poland Road, Glenfield, Auckland 10, New Zealand,
in South Africa by Random House (Pty) Ltd,
Isle of Houghton, Corner Boundary Road & Carse O'Gowrie,
Houghton 2198, South Africa,
and in India by Random House India Pvt Ltd,
301 World Trade Tower, Hotel Intercontinental Grand Complex,
Barakhamba Lane, New Delhi 110001, India

THE RANDOM HOUSE GROUP Limited Reg. No. 954009
www.kidsatrandomhouse.co.uk

A CIP catalogue record for this book is available from the British Library.

Printed and bound in Great Britain by Cox & Wyman. Reading, Berkshire

To:

Robert Bates
Edward Benson
James Bentham
Andrea Boyes
Simon Carney
Clair Feltwell
Mark Hall
Craig Hobson
Elizabeth Holland
Louise Horsley
Andrew Howard
David Jenkinson
Samantha Lee
Gavin Ridealgh
John Robinson
Rachael Rowley
Amanda Whiteley
Victoria Winterburn

Who were there too.
And for Nan, fighting her dragon.

# ROOM 13

I

This is what Fliss dreamed the night before the second year went to Whitby.

She was walking on a road high above the sea. It was dark. She was alone. Waves were breaking at the foot of cliffs to her left, and further out, the moonlight made a silver path on the water.

In front of her was a house. It was a tall house, looming blackly against the sky. There were many windows, all of them dark.

Fliss was afraid. She didn't want to go inside the house. She didn't even want to walk past but she had no control over her feet. They seemed to go by themselves, forcing her on.

She came to a gate. It was made of iron, worked into curly patterns. Near the top was a bit that was supposed to be a bird in flight – a seagull perhaps -- but the gate had been painted black, and the paint had run and hardened into little stalactites along the bird's wings, making it look like a bat.

The gate opened by itself, and as she went through Fliss heard a voice that whispered, 'The Gate of Fate.' She was drawn along a short pathway and up some stone steps to the front door, which also opened by itself. 'The Keep of Sleep,' whispered the voice.

The door closed silently behind her. Moonlight shone coldly through a stained-glass panel into a gloomy hallway. At the far end were stairs that went up into blackness. She didn't want to climb that stairway but her feet drew her along the hallway and up.

She came to a landing with doors. The stairs took a turn and went on up. As Fliss climbed, it grew colder. There was another landing, more doors and another turn in the stair. Upward to a third landing, then a fourth, and then there were no more stairs. She was at the top of the house. There were four doors, each with a number. 10. 11. 12. 13. As she read the numbers, door thirteen swung inward with a squeal. 'No!' she whispered, but it was no use. Her feet carried her over the threshold and the voice hissed, 'The Room of Doom.'

In the room was a table. On the table stood a long, pale box. Fliss thought she knew what it was. It filled her with horror, and she whimpered helplessly as her feet drew her towards it. When she was close she saw a shape in the box and there was a smell like damp earth. When she was very close the voice whispered, 'The Bed of Dread,' and then the shape sat up and reached out for her and she screamed. Her screams woke her and she lay damp and trembling in her bed.

Her mother came and switched on the light and looked down at her. 'What is it, Felicity? I thought I heard you scream.'

Fliss nodded. 'I had a dream, Mum. A nightmare.'

'Poor Fliss.' Her mother sat down on the bed and stroked her hair. 'It's all the excitement, I expect – thinking about going away tomorrow.' She smiled. 'Try to go back to sleep, dear. You've a long day ahead of you.'

Fliss clutched her mother's arm. 'I don't want to go, Mum.'

'What?'

'I don't want to go. I want to drop out of the trip.'

'But why – not just because of a silly dream, surely?'

'Well, yes, I suppose so, Mum. It was about Whitby, I think. A house by the sea.'

'A house?'

'Yes.' She shivered, remembering. 'I was in this house and something horrible was after me. Can I drop out, Mum?'

Her mother sighed. 'I suppose you could, Felicity, if you're as upset as all that. I could ring Mrs Evans first thing, tell her not to expect you, but you might feel differently in the morning.' She smiled. 'Daylight makes us forget our dreams, or else they seem funny – even the scary ones. Let's decide in the morning, eh?'

Fliss smiled wanly. 'OK.' She knew she wouldn't forget her dream, and that it would never seem funny. But it was all right. She was in control of her feet (she wiggled them under the covers to make sure), and they weren't going to take her anywhere she didn't want to go.

If you were a second year there was a different feel about arriving at school that morning. Your friends were standing around in groups by the gate with bags and cases and no uniform, watching the other kids trail down the drive to begin another week of lessons.

You'd be going into school yourself, of course, but only for a few minutes. Only long enough to answer your name and listen to some final instructions from Mr Joyce. There was a coach at the bottom of the drive – a gleaming blue-and-white coach with tinted windows and brilliant chrome, waiting to whisk you beyond the reach of chairs and tables and bells and blackboards and all the sights and sounds and smells of school, to freedom, adventure and the sea. A week. A whole week, tingling with possibilities and bright with promise.

Fliss had changed her mind. Waking to the sun

in her window and birds in the garden, she had thought about her friends, and the sea, and the things which were waiting there, and her dream of the night before had seemed misty and unreal, which of course it was. Her mother had been pleased, and had resisted the temptation to say 'I told you so.'

She'd managed to persuade her parents not to come and see her off. Some parents always did, even when their kids were just off on a day trip. Fliss thought it was daft. Talking in loud voices so everyone could hear, saying stuff like 'Wrap up warm and stay away from the water and don't forget to phone so we'll know you arrived in one piece.' Plonkers.

Lisa Watmough was among the crowd by the gate. She was wearing jeans and talking to a girl called Ellie-May Sunderland. Fliss didn't like Ellie-May much. Nobody did. She was sulky, spoilt and selfish. But never mind. They were off to the seaside, weren't they? Fliss joined them, putting her suitcase on the ground next to Lisa's. 'Hi, you two. Nice morning.'

'Yeah.' They smiled at the sky. 'I can't wait to get on that beach,' said Fliss.

'I can't wait to see the hotel,' said Lisa. 'Mr Hepworth says it's called The Crow's Nest. I hope we're in the same room, Fliss.'

'You won't be,' said Ellie-May. 'Our Shelley went last year and she says Mrs Evans splits you up from your friends so you don't play about at night.'

'She might not this year. It's a different hotel. And anyway, me and Fliss wouldn't play about, would we, Fliss?'

Fliss shook her head and Ellie-May sniggered. 'Try telling Mrs Evans that.'

Lisa looked at her watch. It was nearly ten to nine. 'We'd better move,' she said. 'The sooner we get the boring bit over, the sooner we'll be off.' They picked up their luggage and set off down the drive.

Mr Hepworth was standing by the coach. As the girls approached he called out, 'Come on you three – hurry up. Leave your cases by the back of the bus and go into the hall.' The driver was stowing luggage in the boot, watched by a knot of parents. The three girls deposited their cases and hurried into school.

All the second-year kids were lined up in the hall, waiting for Mr Joyce. As Fliss got into line she felt somebody's breath on her cheek and a voice whispered the word 'Dracula' in her ear. She turned round to find Gary Bazzard grinning at her. She scowled. 'What you on about?'

'I said Dracula.'

'I know that, you div – what about him?'

'Lives in Whitby, doesn't he?'

'Does he naff! He's dead for a start, and when he was alive he lived in Transylvania.'

'No.' The boy shook his shaggy head. 'Whitby. Old Hepworth told us. And he's not dead neither. He's undead. He sleeps in a coffin in the daytime and goes out at night.'

Fliss felt a flicker of unease as the boy's words recalled her dream, but the headmaster appeared at that moment and began to address the assembly. He spoke of rambles, ruins and rock-pools as the sun streamed in through high windows and anticipation shone in the eyes of his listeners, but Fliss gazed at the floor, her lip caught between her teeth.

They were off by twenty-five past nine, growling slowly up the drive while Mr Joyce and a handful of parents stood in a haze of exhaust, waving.

Fliss and Lisa managed to get seats together. Lisa had the one by the window. As the coach turned on to the road she twisted round for a last glimpse of the school. 'Goodbye, Bottomtop!' she cried. 'And good riddance.'

'That'll do, Lisa Watmough.'

Startled, she turned. Mrs Evans was sitting two rows behind, glaring at her through the space between headrests.

'Yes, Miss.' She faced the front, dug Fliss in the ribs and giggled. 'I didn't know she was sitting so close. Where's Mrs Marriott?'

'Back seat, so she can keep an eye on us all. And Mr Hepworth's up there with the driver.'

'Huh! Trust teachers to grab all the best seats. Who's this in front of us?' The tops of two heads

17

showed above the headrests.

'Gary Bazzard and David Trotter. I hope we're nowhere near them in the hotel.'

'You won't be,' said Ellie-May, who was sitting across the aisle from Fliss. 'Our Shelley says they put girls on one floor and boys on another so you don't see each other with nothing on.'

'Our Shelley,' sneered Fliss. 'Our Shelley says this, our Shelley says that. I hope we're not going to have a week of what our Shelley says, Ellie-May.'

'Huh!' Ellie-May tossed her head. 'I was telling you how it'll be, that's all, misery-guts. Anyway, you can naff off if you want to know owt else – you won't get it from me.'

'Good!' Fliss shuffled in her seat, turning as far from Ellie-May as she could, and sat scowling across Lisa at the passing scene.

Lisa looked at her. 'What's up with you?' she hissed. 'We're supposed to be enjoying ourselves and you look like somebody with toothache going into double maths.'

'It's her.' Fliss jerked her head in Ellie-May's direction. 'She gets on my nerves.'

'She was only telling you. You wanted to know if we'd be anywhere near Baz and Trot and she said we won't. What's wrong with that?'

Fliss shrugged. 'Nothing.'

'Well then.'

'I don't feel too good, right? I had this dream last night – a nightmare, and I couldn't sleep after it. And then this morning in the hall, Bazzard starts going on about Dracula. Saying he lives in Whitby, stuff like that, and I wasn't in the mood.'

Lisa pulled a face. 'No need to take it out on other people though, is there? You could go to sleep here, on the coach. Look – the seat tips back. Lie back and shut your eyes. There's nothing to look at anyway, unless you like the middle of Leeds.'

So Fliss pressed the button on the armrest and tipped her seat back, but then the boy in the seat behind yelled out that she was crushing his knees and demanded that she return it to its upright position. When she refused, settling back and closing her eyes, the boy, Grant Cooper, began rhythmically kicking the back of the seat, like somebody beating on a drum. Fliss sighed but kept her eyes closed, saying nothing. As she had anticipated, Mrs Evans soon noticed what the boy was up to. A hand came snaking through the gap between the headrests and grabbed a fistful of his hair. 'Ow!' he yelped. Mrs Evans rose, so that the top part of her face appeared over the seat. She began speaking very quietly to Grant Cooper, punctuating her words by alternately tightening and relaxing her grip on his hair.

'Grant Cooper.' (Squeeze) 'The upholstery on that seat cost a lot of money.' (Squeeze) 'It was fitted to make this coach both smart and comfortable.' (Squeeze) 'It was not provided so that horrible little so-and-sos like you could use it for football practice.' (Squeeze) 'How d'you think your mother would like it if somebody came into your house and started kicking the back of her three-piece suite, eh?' (Squeeze) 'Eh?' (Squeeze) 'Like it, would she?' (Squeeze)

'Please, Miss, no, Miss.' Grant's eyes were watering copiously and his mouth was twisted into a grimace which would not have been out of place in a medieval torture-chamber.

'Well, then,' (Squeeze) 'kindly show the same respect for other people's property that your mother would expect to be shown to hers. All right, Grant Cooper?' (Squeeze)

'Yes, Miss.' The grip loosened. The hand withdrew. Grant slumped, like a man cut down from the whipping-post, and wiped his eyes with the back of his hand. Mrs Evans' face sank from view. Fliss smiled faintly to herself, and drifted off to sleep.

Fliss opened her eyes as the coach swung into a tight turn which nearly catapulted her into the aisle. 'What's happening – where are we?'

'Pickering,' said Lisa. 'We're stopping. You've been asleep ages.'

Fliss looked out. They were rolling on to a big car-park with a wall round it. As the coach stopped, Mr Hepworth stood up at the front. 'This is Pickering,' he said. 'And we are making a toilet stop.' His eyes swept along the coach and locked on to those of a boy near the back. 'A toilet stop, Keith Halliday. Not a shopping stop. Not a sight-seeing stop. Not a "let's buy packets of greasy fish and chips, scoff the lot before Sir sees us and then throw up all over the coach" stop. Have I made myself quite clear?'

'Sir.'

'Right. The toilets,' he pointed, 'are down there at the bottom of this car-park. To get into them, you have to go out on to the pavement. It's a very busy road, and I don't want to see anyone trying to cross it. Neither do I want to see boys going into the ladies' toilet, or girls into the gents'. Have I said something funny, Andrew Roberts?'

'No, Sir.'

'Right.' He looked at his watch. 'It's ten past eleven. The coach will leave here at twenty-five past on the dot. Make sure you're on it, because it's a long walk back to Bradford.'

'When we get back on,' whispered Fliss to Lisa, 'it's my turn for the window seat, right?'

Lisa nodded. 'You feeling better, then?'

'Yes, thanks. I had a lovely sleep.'

'I know. You missed a lot, though. There was this field – a sloping field with millions of poppies in it. The whole field was red. It was ace.'

When Fliss got back on the coach there was no sign of Lisa. She sat down and watched the kids straggling across the tarmac in the warm sunshine. Soon, everybody was back on board except her friend. The driver had started the engine and Mrs Marriott was counting heads when Lisa appeared from behind the toilet block and came hurrying to the coach. As she clambered aboard, Mr Hepworth looked at his watch. 'What time did I say we'd be leaving, Lisa Watmough?'

Some of the children were sniggering and Lisa

blushed. 'Twenty-five past, Sir. I forgot the time, Sir.'

'You forgot the time. Well, for your information it is now twenty-six minutes to twelve, and we'll be lucky if we arrive at the hotel by midday, which is when we are expected. The meal which is being prepared for us might well be ruined, and it will be all your fault, Lisa Watmough.' He bent forward suddenly, peering at her jeans. 'What have you got there?' Something was making a bulge in the pocket of Lisa's jeans and she was trying to conceal it with her hand.

'Nothing, Sir.'

'Take it out and give it to me.'

'It's just this, Sir.' She pulled out an object wrapped in tissue paper and handed it over. The teacher stripped away the wrapping to reveal a green plastic torch in the shape of a dragon. The bulb and its protective glass were in the dragon's gaping mouth. Mr Hepworth held up the torch, using only his thumb and forefinger, and looked at it with an expression of extreme distaste.

'Did you bring this – this thing with you from home, Lisa Watmough?'

'No, Sir.'

'Oh. Then I suppose there's a little kiosk inside the ladies' toilet where patrons can do a bit of shopping. Am I right?'

'No, Sir.'

The teacher frowned. 'Then I'm afraid I don't understand. You didn't bring it from home, and you didn't get it in the ladies'. You haven't been anywhere else, yet here it is. Perhaps you laid it, like a hen lays an egg. Did you?'

'No, Sir.'

'Then what did you do?'

'I went in a shop, Sir.'

'You did what?'

'Went in a shop, Sir.'

'And what had I said about shopping, Lisa Watmough, just before you got off the coach?'

'We weren't to do any, Sir.'

'Right. Then why did you go into that shop?'

'I don't know, Sir.'

'You don't know, and neither do I, but here's something I do know. This evening, when the rest of the group is listening to a story in the hotel lounge, you will be in your room writing two apologies – one to the children for having kept them waiting, and one to me for having disobeyed my instructions. When both apologies have been written to my satisfaction, this torch will be returned to you. In the meantime you can leave it with me. Go to your seat.'

'What the heck did you do that for?' whispered Fliss, as Lisa slid into her seat. Lisa was one of those girls who seldom step out of line and are rarely in trouble at school.

She shook her head miserably. 'I don't know, Fliss. I don't even need a torch – I've got a better one at home. You'll think I'm crazy, but I couldn't help it – it was as though my feet were going by themselves.'

'Oh, don't you start,' groaned Fliss.

'What d'you mean?'

'Nothing. Forget it.' She looked out of the window. They passed a sign. North Yorkshire Moors National Park. The coach was climbing. Fliss gazed out as green pasture gave way to tree-less desolation. She shivered.

5

'Hey look!'

A boy on the right-hand side near the front of the coach stood up and pointed. Everybody looked. Out of the bleak landscape rose three white, dome-shaped objects, like gigantic mushrooms breaking through the earth. As the coach carried them closer, they saw a scatter of low buildings and a fence. The great spheres, gleaming in the sunlight, looked like objects in a science-fiction movie.

'Wow! What are they, Sir?'

Mr Hepworth got up. 'That's the Fylingdales early-warning station,' he told them. 'Inside those domes is radar equipment, operated by the British and American forces. It maintains a round-the-clock watch for incoming missiles. They say it would give us a three-minute warning.' He smiled wryly. 'Three minutes in which to do whatever we haven't done yet and always wanted to.'

'What would you do, Sir?' asked a grinning Waseem Kader.

'What would I do?' The teacher thought for a moment. 'I think I'd get a brick and throw it through the biggest window I could find.' He smiled. 'I've always fancied that.'

'Oh, I wouldn't, Sir – I'd run to the Chinese and get chicken chop-suey ten times and gobble it right quick.'

'Yeah!' cried Sarah-Jane Potts. 'That's what I'd do and all – we wouldn't have to pay, would we, Sir?'

'I'd get a big club and smash our Shelley's head in,' said Ellie-May. 'I hate her.'

'There'd be no point, fathead!' sneered a boy behind her. 'She'd be dead in three minutes anyway.'

The noise level rose. Excited voices called back and forth across the coach as everybody tried to outdo everybody else in what they'd do with their last three minutes. The fact that many of them would have needed several hours or even days to carry out their plans was disregarded, and the discussion continued till the vehicle topped the highest rise and Mrs Marriott raised her voice, drawing everybody's attention to the ruins of Whitby Abbey, which were now visible in the hazy distance.

27

Gary Bazzard knelt, leering at Fliss over the back of his seat. 'See – that's where Dracula lives – in the ruins. Old Hepworth told us.'

'Old Hepworth told you no such thing.'

The boy's remark had coincided with a lull in conversation as everybody strained for a glimpse of the abbey, and Mr Hepworth had heard it. 'Old Hepworth told you that Bram Stoker, who created the character of Dracula, was inspired to do so after having seen the ruined abbey. Dracula does not live there or anywhere else. He is a figment of Stoker's imagination, Gary Bazzard, and sometimes I wish the same might be said of you.'

There was laughter at this. The boy's cheeks reddened as he resumed his seat. Fliss smiled faintly, gazing out at the distant ruins and beyond them to the sea.

It was ten past twelve when the coach drew up outside The Crow's Nest Hotel. Mr and Mrs Wilkinson, who ran it, were standing on the top step waiting for them. Lisa flushed, remembering what Mr Hepworth had said about it being all her fault. She hoped he wouldn't point her out to the Wilkinsons as the culprit.

'Check under your seats and on the luggage rack,' warned Mrs Marriott, as everybody stood up. 'Don't leave any of your property in the coach.' The children checked, then filed slowly along the

28

aisle and down on to the pavement. It was sunny, but a breeze blew from the sea, making it cooler than it would now be in Bradford. The driver went round the back and started unloading bags and cases, which their owners quickly claimed.

Fliss looked at the hotel. There was something vaguely familiar about the steps. The porch. Even the breeze, and the distant sound of the sea.

When everybody had their luggage Mr Hepworth led them into the hotel. Fliss looked at the iron bird on the black gate. For a moment she thought it was meant to be a gull, but then she remembered the name of the place and decided it was probably a crow. Somebody had made a poor job of painting it. Drips had run down to the edges of its wings and hardened there, giving them a webbed, spiky appearance, so that it looked more like a bat than a bird.

'Right, listen!'

Lunch over, they had crammed themselves into the lounge with all their baggage, squeezing into chairs and settees, perching on the edges of tables, sitting on bags and cases on the floor while the three teachers sorted out room allocations and other matters with the Wilkinsons in the hall-way. They had taken in the view from the bay window, looked at the prints round the walls and were starting to get restless when Mr Hepworth stuck his head through the doorway.

'I'm waiting, Andrew Roberts.' The noise faded as Andrew Roberts stopped using the top of his suitcase as a drum and everybody looked towards the teacher. 'There are bedrooms on four floors in this hotel, and two rooms to a floor. I'm going to give you your room numbers now, and tell you which floor your room is on. As soon as you know your floor and number, I want you to pick up your luggage and walk quietly up to your room. What do I want you to do, Gemma Carlisle?'

'Sir, go up to our room, Sir.'

'And how do I want you to go?'

'Walking quietly, Sir.'

'Right.' Mr Hepworth glared about the crowded room from under dark, bushy eyebrows. 'Walking quietly. Not charging up the stairs like a crazed rhinoceros, swinging your case, smashing vases and screaming at the top of your voice. And when you find your room, go in and wait. Don't touch anything, and don't start fighting about whose bed is which, or who's going to have this wardrobe or that drawer. The teacher responsible for your floor will come and sort all that out as soon as possible.' He put on his spectacles and began reading from a list.

'Joanne O'Connor, Maureen O'Connor, Felicity Morgan and Marie Nero, top floor, room ten.'

'Aw, Sir – '

'Moaning already, Felicity?'

'Me and Lisa wanted to be together, Sir.'

'Well you're not, are you? We'd be here all day if we started trying to put everybody with their best friend. Off you go.' He scanned his list again. 'Vicky Holmes, Samantha Storey and Lisa Watmough, top floor, room eleven.'

Fliss carried her case up the stairs. There were brown photographs in frames all the way up. Ships and boats with sails. Old-time fisherfolk in bulky clothes. A wave breaking over a jetty.

Room ten contained a pair of bunk-beds and a double bed. There were two wardrobes, a chest of drawers and a dressing-table. The carpet was green and thin. A small washbasin stood in one corner. A brown photograph on the wall showed two children playing with a toy boat in a rock-pool.

Maureen went to the window. 'Hey! We're ever so high. You can see the sea from here.' Joanne and Marie went to look. Fliss put her case down and joined them. Beyond the road an expanse of close-mown grass, bisected by a footpath, stretched almost to the clifftop. There were wooden seats at intervals along the footpath. Away to the left was something which might be a crazy-golf course, while to the right stood a shelter with benches and large windows, and a telephone kiosk. In the shelter an old woman sat. She was dressed in black, and seemed to be looking straight at them. Beyond all this, glinting blue-grey under the sun, lay the sea.

'Isn't it lovely?' breathed Marie.

'Hmm.' Maureen's eyes followed a gull that swooped and soared along the line of the cliff. Joanne peered towards the horizon and thought she could make out the long, low shape of a ship – a tanker, perhaps.

Fliss gazed out to sea too, but she wasn't looking for a ship. She was thinking, Marie's right. It is lovely, but not nearly so beautiful as at night, when the moon makes a silver path across the water.

Behind them somebody knocked loudly on the door and flung it open. 'Hey, Fliss!' It was Lisa. 'We're right next door – come and see our room.'

Fliss was starting towards the door when Mrs Marriott's voice sounded on the landing. 'What are you doing there, Lisa Watmough? Didn't you hear Mr Hepworth say you were to wait in your room?'

'Yes, Miss.' There was a scampering noise. Lisa's face disappeared. Fliss waited a moment then looked out. There was nobody on the landing. The door of number eleven was half-open, and she heard Mrs Marriott asking Lisa if she didn't think she'd caused enough trouble for one day.

There were two other doors. One had twelve on it, and Fliss guessed that was the bathroom. The other had no number, but she knew what number it would have if it had. She was gazing at it, wondering what sort of room it concealed when Mrs Marriott came out of number eleven.

'Why are you standing there, Felicity Morgan?' she enquired.

'Please, Miss, I was just wondering what sort of room that is.' She pointed to the numberless door.

The teacher glanced at it. 'Linen cupboard, I should think.'

'It's big for a cupboard, Miss.'

The teacher nodded. 'Hotels need big cupboards, Felicity. All those sheets. Or it could be a broom cupboard, I suppose. Anyway, let's get your room organized.'

Felicity got the bottom bunk. She was glad. She hadn't fancied sharing the double bed. Mrs Marriott put Joanne and Maureen in that. They were twins, so that was all right. Marie had the top bunk. They had half an hour to unpack, put their things away and tidy up, then everybody was going down to the seafront for a look around.

Excited, anxious to be off, Fliss's three companions worked quickly. They chattered and giggled, but Fliss was silent. She was wondering when it was that she'd seen the sea under the moon, and noticing how broom rhymes with room, and also with doom.

It was three o'clock when the children gathered on the pavement outside the hotel. There were thirty-one of them, and Mr Hepworth split them into two groups of ten and one of eleven, with girls and boys in each group. 'Remember your group,' he said, 'because we'll be in groups a lot of the time while we're here.' Fliss found herself in Mrs Evans' group, and to her disgust Gary Bazzard was in it too. Gary was pretty disgusted himself, because his best friend David Trotter had ended up in Mrs Marriott's group. Lisa was in that group too.

It was breezy, but sunny and quite warm. The groups set off at intervals, turning right and walking in twos down North Terrace towards Captain Cook's monument and the whalebone arch. Fliss's group went second. As they passed the shelter, Fliss saw that the old woman was still there. She was gazing towards the hotel and seemed to be talking to herself. The first group was looking at the monument, so Mrs Evans led them to the arch.

'Now: can anybody tell me why there should be a whalebone arch at Whitby?' she asked. 'Yes, Roger?'

'For people to walk through, Miss.'

'Yes, Roger, I know it's for people to walk through, but why should it be made from whalebone? Anybody?'

Tara Matejak raised her hand. She was Fliss's partner. 'Miss, because there were whaling ships at Whitby in the olden days.'

'That's right, Tara. And who knows why whales were valuable? Roger?'

'Oil, Miss. They used whale-oil for margarine and lamps and that. And they used the bones for women's dresses, Miss.'

'That's right.' Mrs Evans shielded her eyes with her hand and squinted up at the arch. 'What part of the whale's skeleton is this arch made from, d'you think?'

'Its jawbones, Miss,' said Maureen.

'Right. And they've put something on top, haven't they – it looks like an arrow. Can anybody guess what it actually is?'

Everybody gazed up at the object but nobody answered. After a moment Mrs Evans said, 'Well,

I'm not absolutely sure, but it looks to me like the tip of a harpoon. An old-fashioned harpoon – the sort they threw by hand from the bows of a whaleboat. Who's read *Moby Dick*?'

'Miss, I've seen *Jaws* on the telly.'

'What on earth has that got to do with it, Richard Varley?'

'Miss, nothing, Miss.'

'Then don't be so stupid, you silly boy!'

Nobody had read *Moby Dick*.

Mr Hepworth's group was now approaching, so Mrs Evans led Fliss and the others to Captain Cook's monument. They surrounded it, looking at the lengthy inscriptions on its plinth.

'Who can tell us something about Captain Cook?'

'Miss, he had one eye and one arm.'

'Rubbish, Michael Tostevin! That was Lord Nelson. Yes, Joanne?'

'He had a peg leg, Miss, and a parrot on his shoulder.'

'That was Long John Silver, dear – a fictitious character.' Mrs Evans sounded tired.

When they'd finished with Captain Cook, they went down a flight of stone steps on to a road called the Khyber Pass, and from there to the sea-front. There, Mrs Evans turned them loose for a while to join their classmates on the sands, while she sank on to a bench which already supported her two colleagues.

Fliss found Lisa at the water's edge. 'What d'you think of it so far?'

Lisa pulled a face. 'Dead captains. Dead whales. Dead boring.'

Fliss laughed. 'It's OK down here though, isn't it?'

Lisa nodded. 'You bet. Let's find some flat pebbles and play at skimming.'

They played on the sand for an hour or so, until
Mr Hepworth called them together at the foot of
the slipway which connected the promenade with
the beach.

'Right. What I thought we'd do between now
and teatime is this: walk along the road here and
have a look at the fish quay, then along the quayside to the swing-bridge and over into the old
town. There are lots of interesting shops in the
old town, including some specializing in Whitby
jet. We could have a look in some of the windows,
but I don't think we should shop today – otherwise some of us might run out of pocket-money
halfway through the week. At the end of the old
town is a flight of steps leading up to the abbey
and a church. There are a lot of steps, and I want
you to count them as we go up and tell me how
many there are. We'll go in groups again – d'you
know your group, Barry Tune?'

'Sir.'

'Good. Here we go, then.'

The three teachers moved apart and called their groups to them. The children got into twos, and this time Fliss had Gary for a partner. He grinned at her. 'Holding hands, are we?'

'No chance. I've to eat my tea with this hand when we get back.'

'I'll be using a knife and fork.'

'Ha, ha, ha.'

They looked at the fish dock, but there were no boats in and the sheds with their stacks of fish-boxes were shut. They went along the quayside, threading their way between strolling holiday-makers, looking in shop windows or at the different kinds of boats in the harbour. There was that exciting smell in the air which you get at the seaside – that blend of salt and mud and fish and sweet rottenness which has you breathing deeply and makes you tingle.

They were taking their time – the evening meal was not until six-thirty – and Fliss was looking at a coble with her name, *Felicity*, painted on its prow when Gary grabbed her hand and cried, 'Hey – look at this!'

'What?' She spoke irritably and jerked her hand away, but looked where he pointed and saw a narrow building with dark windows and a sign which said 'The Dracula Experience'. A tall man with a pale face, dressed all in black, smiled from the doorway at the passing group. His teeth seemed quite ordinary.

Gary raised his hand and waved it at Mrs Evans. 'Miss – can we go in here, Miss, please?'

Mrs Evans, who had been looking out over the harbour, turned. She saw the building, read the sign, smiled faintly and shook her head. 'Not just now, Gary. On Thursday, everybody will be given some free time to shop for presents and spend what's left of their money in whatever way they choose. You'll be able to buy yourself some Dracula Experience then.' She looked into the eyes of the smiling man and added, loudly, 'If you must.'

They crossed the bridge and sauntered through the narrow streets of the old town till they came to the church steps. By the time they reached the top, Fliss was out of breath. She'd counted a hundred and ninety-seven steps but Mr Hepworth, whose group had got there first, said there were a hundred and ninety-nine and she believed him.

The top of the steps gave on to an old graveyard. Weathered stones leaned at various angles, so eroded you couldn't read the epitaphs. Long grass rippled in the wind. There was a church, and a breathtaking view of Whitby and the sea.

They had a look inside the church. It was called St Mary's. Mr Hepworth pointed out its special features. You could buy postcards and souvenirs by the door. Fliss bought a postcard of the ruined abbey to send home. When they were gathered outside she said, 'Are we going to the ruins, Sir?' She wasn't sure whether she wanted to or not.

'Not today, Felicity. We'll be looking at them on Wednesday morning, before we set off to walk to Saltwick Bay.'

They poked about in the churchyard for a while and visited the toilets near the abbey. Then they descended the hundred and ninety-nine steps and began making their way back to The Crow's Nest. The fresh air and exercise had sharpened everybody's appetite, and most of the children spent the walk back wondering what was for tea. Fliss did not. She was thinking about the landing at the top of the house, and what it would be like in the dark. The funny thing was, she seemed to know.

They got back in plenty of time for tea, which was eggs, chips and sausages, with swiss-roll and ice-cream for pudding. Afterwards everybody went upstairs to put on tracksuits and trainers. Mrs Marriott was taking them for a game of rounders on the sands. Lisa would be missing out, because of the apologies she had to write.

Gary Bazzard's room was one floor below Fliss's. Number seven. When she came down the stairs he was standing in the doorway showing something to a group of his friends, who were making admiring noises. As Fliss passed he called out, 'How about this, Fliss?'

She glanced in his direction. He was holding up the biggest stick of rock she'd ever seen. She didn't like him much, and would have loved to walk on with her nose in the air, but the pink stick really was enormous: nearly a metre long and about four centimetres thick. She stopped. 'Where the heck did you get that from?' she asked, in what she hoped was a scornful voice.

'Shop on the quay. One pound fifty. No one saw me 'cause I stuck it down my jeans' leg.' His friends gasped and chuckled at his daring.

Fliss pulled a face. 'You're nuts. One pound fifty? I wouldn't give you fifty pence for it.'

'You wouldn't get chance.'

'It'll rot your teeth, so there.'

'You're only jealous.'

'I'm not. I hope Mr Hepworth catches you and hits you on the head with it.'

It was a good game of rounders. It was more fun than it might have been, because the tide was coming in and the strip of sand they were playing on grew narrower and narrower. People kept hitting the ball into the sea, and some of the fielders had to play barefoot so that they could retrieve it. Finally the pitch became so restricted that play was impossible. They wrapped up the game, retreated to the top of one of the concrete buttresses which protected the foot of the cliff and sat, watching the tide come in.

Cocoa and biscuits were served in the lounge at half-past eight. The children sat sipping and munching while twilight fell outside and Mrs Evans read them a story. Lisa came down with her written apologies. Mr Hepworth read them, nodded, and gave her back her torch. It was nine o'clock. Bedtime.

Fliss was tired, but she couldn't sleep. It was fun at first, lying in the dark, talking with Marie and the twins, but one by one they drifted off to sleep and she was left listening to the muffled noises that rose from the boys' room below. After a while these too stopped, and then there was only the occasional creak, and the rhythmic shush of the sea.

She lay staring at the ceiling, waiting for her eyes to get tired. If the lids grew heavy enough they'd close, and then she'd drift off. She wouldn't even know she was lying in the dark, and when she woke up it would be morning and the first night – the worst night – would be over.

Phantom lights swam across her field of vision, lazily, like shoals of tiny fish. She watched them, but they failed to lull her, and presently it came to her that she would have to go to the bathroom.

She listened. If somebody else was awake somewhere it would be easier. A boy on the floor below perhaps, or one of the teachers. She looked at her watch. 23.56. Four minutes to midnight. Surely somebody was still about – the Wilkinsons, locking up for the night, or Mr Hepworth making a final patrol.

Silence. In all the world, only Fliss was awake.

She listened to the steady breathing of the other three girls. Why couldn't one of them have been a snorer? If somebody had been snoring she could have given them a shake. A policeman going by outside would be better than nothing – his footsteps might make her feel safe. But there was no policeman. There wasn't even a car.

The bed creaked as she sat up and swung her legs out. She listened. Nothing. The steady breathing continued. She hadn't disturbed anybody. Perhaps she'd have to put the light on to find the door – that would wake them. But no. There was moonlight and the curtains were thin and she could see quite clearly. It would be most unfair to wake them with the light.

She stood up and crept towards the door. There was sand in the carpet. A floorboard creaked and she paused, hopefully. One of the twins stirred, mumbling, and Fliss whispered, 'Maureen? Joanne?' but there was no response.

She opened the door a crack and looked out. The only illumination came from a small window on the half-landing below. It was minimal. She could make out the dark shapes of the doors but not the pattern on the carpet. The air had a musty smell and felt cold.

As she hesitated for a moment in the doorway, peering into the gloom and listening, she became aware of a faint sound – the snuffling, grunting noise of somebody snoring beyond the door of room eleven. She found it oddly reassuring, and crossed the landing quickly in case it should stop.

Re-crossing a minute later with the hiss of the toilet cistern in her ears, she could still hear it. It seemed louder, and was accompanied now by a thin, whimpering noise, like crying. Fliss pulled a face. Somebody feeling homesick. Not Lisa, surely?

The idea that her friend might be in distress made her forget her fear for a moment. She took a couple of steps towards room eleven, unsure of what she intended to do. As she did so, she became aware that the noise was not coming from that room at all, but from the one next to it – the cupboard. Her eyes flicked to its door. On it, visible in the midnight gloom, was the number thirteen.

She recoiled, covering her mouth with her hand. When she had asked Mrs Marriott what lay beyond that door, there had been no number on it. She knew there hadn't, yet there it was. Thirteen. And somebody was in there. Somebody, or some thing.

She backed away. The hissing of the cistern dwindled and ceased. The other sounds continued, and now the whimpering was more persistent, and

47

the snuffling had a viscous quality to it, like a pig rooting in mud.

She retreated slowly, holding her breath. When she reached the doorway of her own room she backed through it, feeling for the doorknob and keeping her eyes fixed on the door of room thirteen. Once inside, she closed the door quickly, crossed to her bed and lay staring at the ceiling while spasms shook her body.

Much later, when the shivering had stopped and she was drifting to sleep, she thought she heard stealthy footsteps on the landing, but when she woke at seven with the sun in her face and her friends' excited chatter in her ears, she wondered whether she might have dreamed it all.

## 10

They gathered in the lounge after breakfast. Mr Hepworth had fixed a large map of the coast to the wall. He pointed. 'Here's Whitby, where we are. And here,' he slid his finger northward along the coastline, 'is Staithes, where the coach will drop us this morning. Staithes used to be an important fishing port like Whitby, and there are still a few fishermen there, but it is a quiet village now. Captain Cook worked in a shop at Staithes when he was very young – before he decided to be a sailor.'

'Will we be going in the shop, Sir?'

'No, Neil Atkinson, we will not. Unfortunately, it was washed away by the sea a long time ago. However, if we are very lucky we might see a ghost.'

There were gasps and exclamations at this. 'Captain Cook's ghost, Sir?' asked James Garside. The teacher shook his head, smiling. 'No, James.

Not Captain Cook's. A young girl's. There's a dangerous cliff at Staithes, a crumbling cliff, and the story goes that when this girl was walking under it one day, a chunk of rock fell and decapitated her. Who knows what decapitated means? Yes, Steven Jackson?'

'Sir, knocked her cap off, Sir.'

'No. Michelle Webster?'

'Squashed her, Sir?'

'Closer, but not right. 'Ellie-May Sunderland?'

'Sir, knocked her head off, Sir.'

'Correct.' He leaned forward, peering at the girl through narrowed eyes. 'Are you all right, Ellie-May – you look a bit pasty?'

'Yes, Sir.'

'Sure?'

'Yes, Sir.'

'Right. Well, there's a bridge over a creek at Staithes, and that's where the headless ghost has been seen. We'll be having a look round the village, then walking along the clifftop path to Runswick Bay. That's here.' He jabbed at the map again. A boy raised his hand.

'What is it, Robert Field?'

'How far is it, Sir?'

The teacher shrugged, smiling. 'A few miles. We'll find somewhere to eat our packed lunches on the way, and the coach will be waiting at

Runswick to bring us back here. Right – it's a lovely sunny morning, so let's get started.'

Lisa saved Fliss a seat on the coach. As they roared along the coast road she said, 'We stayed awake ever so late in our room last night, talking. Telling jokes and that. It was brilliant.'

'You were all asleep before midnight, though,' said Fliss.

'How d'you know?'

'I passed your door at midnight. There wasn't a sound.'

'What were you doing, passing our door at midnight?'

'I went to the toilet. Or at least I think I did.'

'How d'you mean, you think you did – don't you know?'

Fliss pulled a face. 'No. It's all mixed up with this horrible dream I had.'

'What was it about, your dream?'

Fliss told her friend about the strange noises that had seemed to come from the linen cupboard, the number thirteen on the door, the footsteps she thought she'd heard later. 'It all seemed so real, Lisa. But then this morning I looked, and of course there was no number on the door and the sun was shining and everybody was shouting and messing about on the landing, and it didn't seem real any more. D'you know what I mean?'

Lisa nodded. 'Sure. It was all a dream – you didn't go to the toilet and you weren't outside our door at midnight so you don't know what time we went to sleep, right?'

'Right. Except –'

'Except what, Fliss? What is it?'

'After the toilet, I dreamed I washed my hands, right? And it was one of those spurty taps where the water comes all at once and goes everywhere. Some went on the floor. Quite a lot, in fact. There didn't seem to be anything to mop it up with, and anyway I was too scared to hang about so I left it.'

Lisa shrugged. 'Dream water in a dream bathroom. So what?'

Fliss looked at her friend. 'It was still there this morning,' she said.

They spent an hour in Staithes, but nobody saw the ghost. They saw crab pots piled by cottage doors and boats tied up in the creek. They stared at the dangerous cliff and tried to imagine what it would be like to be walking along quite normally one second, and to have no head the next. They bought sweets and ice-lollies and stood among their knapsacks and shoulder-bags, chatting and watching the waves while the teachers had a cup of tea. At eleven o'clock they picked up their bags and moved out, leaving the village by way of a steep, winding footpath which led to the clifftop and on out of sight. Mr Hepworth said, 'This is part of the Cleveland Way, and it will take us to Runswick Bay. It's a three–mile walk, more or less. About halfway, we'll stop and eat our lunches. There's no tearing hurry, but do try to keep up – the path runs very close to the cliff edge in places, and if there are stragglers it becomes difficult to keep an eye on everybody. Are you listening, John Phelan?'

'Yessir.'

'Good. Off we go, then.'

The sun was a fuzzy ball above the sea. Little white clouds sailed inland on the breeze, their shadows racing across a rolling landscape of wheat field and meadow. Strung out in twos and threes along the track, the children walked and chattered. Gulls wheeled and soared, or floated like scraps of paper on the water far below. A jet, miles high, drew a thin white line across the sky.

Lisa flung out her arms and laughed. 'Lovely!' she cried. 'Don't you think it's lovely, Fliss – the smells? All this space?'

Fliss nodded. 'I was just thinking about the others, stuck in school having boring lessons, and us here enjoying ourselves.' She looked at her watch. 'We'd be in French now.'

'Did you have to mention that?' scowled Lisa. 'Trying to spoil my day, I know.'

'No, I'm not. I think it makes it better, thinking about where you'd be if you weren't here. It makes you appreciate it more.'

'Yeah, well, I can appreciate it without having to think about French, thank you very much. Are you still bothered about that dream, by the way?'

Fliss looked at her friend. 'Now who's trying to

spoil whose day?' She thought for a while. 'No,
I'm not worried. Not at the moment. Not here.
It's like I told you – in broad daylight all that sort
of stuff seems daft. You say to yourself, it was just
a dream, and you believe it. It's when you're in
bed at night and everything's quiet that you start
wondering. Anyway, I don't want to think about
it now. What kind of bird's that?' She pointed.
'The black one with a grey head. I've seen a few
of them today.'

Lisa shrugged. 'I don't know. I'm no good at
birds. Ask Mrs Evans.'

Fliss looked behind. 'Where is Mrs Evans – I
thought she was walking at the back?'

'She was. We must be going too fast for her or
something. Either that or she's fallen off the cliff.
Anyway, you could ask Mrs Marriott instead –
she's just up there.'

Fliss giggled. 'You mean it doesn't matter if
Mrs Evans has fallen into the sea, because she's
not the only one who can identify birds?'

'No, you div – I never said that. Anyway,
she won't have fallen, will she? We've left her
behind, that's all. She hasn't kept up like old
Hepworth said – I wonder if he'll make her write
an apology?'

'Will he heck! D'you think we should tell somebody?'

'Can if you want. Mrs Marriott's just up there.'

Fliss put on a spurt, swerved past Helen Smith and Robert Field, and touched the teacher's shoulder.

'Miss.'

Mrs Marriott turned her head. 'What is it, Felicity?'

'We can't see Mrs Evans, Miss. She was at the back, and now she's disappeared. We thought we should mention it, Miss.'

'Hmm.' Mrs Marriott looked back over the quarter mile or so of track which was visible from where they were standing. Children passed them, leaving the path to do so. 'Thank you, Felicity. D'you think you could catch up with Mr Hepworth – tell him I sent you and ask him to stop the walk? She's probably just fallen behind, but I think perhaps we ought to wait for her.'

'Yes, Miss.'

She set off along the track, weaving in and out among her classmates. One or two called after her, demanding to know where she thought she was going or what the rush was about but she ignored them, going at a steady jog and keeping her eyes on Mr Hepworth.

She was still a couple of hundred metres behind him when he stopped and looked back. She waved and shouted, 'Sir – Sir!' and to her relief he raised his hand, halting the column, and stood watching her approach.

'What is it, Felicity?' he asked, as she came panting up to him. She told him and he shaded his eyes with his hand, peering back the way they'd come.

'Hmm. Well. She's nowhere in sight – probably twisted an ankle or something and fallen behind. We'll wait here a minute or two, and if she doesn't show up I'll go back and have a look.'

The line shortened, as those further back caught up and stopped. The children milled about, wondering what was happening, and a girl called out, 'Is this where we eat our lunch, Sir?'

Mr Hepworth shook his head. 'No, Samantha Varley, it is not. We're waiting for Mrs Evans, who has fallen behind a bit.' He said something quietly to Mrs Marriott, who came along the line counting heads.

'One missing,' she called. 'Is it Ellie-May? I don't think I've seen her.'

'It is, Miss,' said Haley Denton. 'I saw her dropping back, ages ago.'

'That's probably it, then,' said Mr Hepworth. 'Ellie-May fell behind and Mrs Evans is walking with her. I thought she wasn't looking too bright, back at the hotel.' He looked at his watch. 'We'll give them five minutes, then I'll set off back. Take your packs off and sit down – we might as well take a breather while we can.'

Fliss went back to sit with Lisa, but she hadn't been sitting for more than a minute when one of the boys yelled, 'They're coming, Sir!'

Everybody watched as the two figures approached. When they reached the place where Fliss and Lisa were sitting, Mrs Evans said, 'Now then, Ellie-May. You sit with Felicity and Lisa. They'll look after you.' She smiled, putting Ellie-May's knapsack, which she'd been carrying, on the grass. 'Ellie-May's not feeling very well, girls. You'll look after her, won't you?'

'Yes, Miss.'

'I knew you would.' She smiled again and moved on, murmuring, 'Sensible girls. Nice, sensible girls.'

Ellie-May looked awful. Her cheeks were white and there were dark smudges, like bruises, under her eyes. She sat down. 'I couldn't keep up,' she growled. 'I tried, but I went all dizzy. Silly Mrs Evans made me sit with my head between my knees for a bit and I had to drink tea from her flask. It tasted awful. As soon as I felt a bit better we set off after you at about fifty miles an hour, and now I feel rotten again.'

'Mrs Evans is nice,' said Lisa. 'She carried your pack, didn't she? What's the matter with you anyway – tummy bug or something?'

Ellie-May scowled. 'I don't know, do I, fat-head? Why do you ask such stupid questions?'

'Hey, Sunderland!' A group of boys was sitting nearby. One of them, David Trotter, grinned across at Ellie-May. 'If you didn't go creeping about in the middle of the night, we wouldn't have to hang around waiting for you when we're supposed to be out walking.'

Ellie-May shook her head. 'I don't know what you're talking about. I don't creep around. I was asleep all night.'

'Ooh, you lying so-and-so! I saw you. Half-past two, it was. You'd been to the top floor. You came down on to our landing and disappeared down the stairs. I was watching you from the bathroom.'

'No, you weren't, you spaz. You couldn't. I never left the room, so there!'

'Blue pyjamas with rabbits on, right?'

'Shut up. I don't know what you're on about.'

'I'm on about your pyjamas. You've got blue ones with rabbits on, haven't you?

'So what?'

'So how would I know that if I didn't see you?'

'I dunno. Maybe you were on the stairs or something when I was getting ready for bed. Maybe it's you that creeps about in the night.'

Fliss sat chewing on a grass stalk, gazing out to sea. She was thinking about last night. The noises from the cupboard. The footsteps. Lisa had said it was a dream and she'd tried to believe it was, but there was the water on the bathroom floor, and now this. She'd heard footsteps in the small hours, and Ellie-May had been seen coming down the stairs in pyjamas. Pyjamas with rabbits on them. So maybe it wasn't a dream, but if it wasn't a dream what was it? Had Ellie-May been in the cupboard last night? Was that possible? It was where the noises had come from, but then what about the number? If the noises were real so was the number, yet it wasn't there this morning. And anyway, why would anyone be in a cupboard at two in the morning? The whole thing was crazy. Unless –

She shivered.

12

'Right – this'll do nicely,' said Mr Hepworth. They'd reached a grassy hollow where the land ran down in a gentle slope to a cliff which was neither sheer nor high. The grass was very green and quite short, and the children sat down on it and took out their lunch-packs. Friends sat together, and the three teachers found a spot near the top of the slope from which they could see what everybody was doing.

Fliss grabbed Lisa's elbow and steered her away from the group she'd been about to join. 'I've got to talk to you,' she hissed. Ellie-May stood, wondering whether to go with them or stay with the group. Fliss turned and called, 'See you in a bit, Ellie-May – OK?'

Ellie-May nodded. 'Sure.' She sat down between Haley and Bobby Tuke. If people didn't want her around she wasn't going to worry about it.

'What's up?' said Lisa, when they'd got settled.

61

Fliss swallowed a mouthful of fishpaste sand-wich. 'You heard what Trotter said back there. About her?' She nodded towards Ellie-May, who was sitting with her back to them.

Lisa nodded. 'I think he made it up. He's like that.'

Fliss shook her head. 'I don't. I heard footsteps, didn't I? I think it was Ellie-May, and I think she was in that cupboard when I went to the bath-room.'

Her friend looked at her. 'Don't be silly, Fliss! It was a dream. Why would Ellie-May sit in a cup-board in the middle of the night, making funny noises? Why would anybody? And how could a door have a number on it at midnight, and none in the morning? You're barmy.'

'No, I'm not. What about the water on the bath-room floor?'

'Anybody could have squirted water on the floor. People do it on purpose, don't they?'

'Well, what about Ellie-May, then – what d'you think's wrong with her?'

Lisa shrugged. I dunno. I'm not a doctor, am I? Maybe she's got food-poisoning, which we all will after these rotten sandwiches.' She pulled a face, chewing. 'Why – what do you think's wrong, Doctor Morgan?'

'I think something happened to her in that

cupboard. I wasn't dreaming at all. I know that now. I'm off over to talk to Trot.'

She got up and went over to where David Trotter was sitting with a group of his friends. The boys stopped talking at her approach and squinted up at her, shielding their eyes with their hands. 'What do you want, mong-features?' asked Gary Bazzard, through a mouthful of something pink. Fliss ignored him. 'Can I have a word please, Trot?'

'Trot!' whooped Richard Varley. 'What is she, Trot – your girlfriend or something?'

Trotter blushed. 'Is she heck.' He scowled up at Fliss. 'What about?'

'I'll tell you over there.' She nodded towards a vacant spot on the slope. The others laughed. 'Watch her, Trot,' said Bazzard, 'she's after you.'

The red-faced boy scrambled to his feet. 'Come on then,' he growled. 'And it better be important or I'll chuck you off the cliff.'

They moved away from the others, and Fliss told him what she'd seen and heard in the night, linking it with what he'd seen and with Ellie-May's present condition. The boy glanced across at Ellie-May once or twice while she was speaking, and when she'd finished he nodded. 'OK. It all fits, and she looks rough, no doubt about that. But what I don't get is, why would she go up two

63

floors and into a cupboard in the first place, and if she did, and something happened to her there – something bad – why hasn't she told one of the teachers?'

Fliss shrugged. 'I don't know, Trot, but there's something funny going on, isn't there?'

'Maybe. But what d'you want me to do about it?'

'I don't want you to do anything. Not by yourself. I'm thinking of keeping watch tonight to see if Ellie-May goes walkabout again. I think Lisa will join me. Will you?'

'I dunno. It seems daft to me. I mean, a cupboard. I ask you – what could there be in a cupboard, Felicity?'

'Fliss.'

'What?'

'Fliss. Call me Fliss.'

'Oh, I see. What could be in a cupboard, Fliss?'

'Who knows?' She chuckled. 'The point is, dare you keep watch with us and find out?'

'How d'you mean, dare I? D'you think I'm scared or something?'

'Could be.'

'Well, I'm not, I can tell you that.'

'Prove it. Watch with us.'

'OK, if Gary can come too.'

'How d'you know he wants to?'

'I don't, yet. He doesn't know anything about it, but he'll want to be in on it when he does. Can I tell him?'

Fliss sighed. 'I suppose so. But get him by himself, right? We don't want the whole flipping class stampeding around in the middle of the night, or nothing will happen at all.'

The boy smiled. 'I don't think it will anyway.'

'Well, we'll see, won't we?' said Fliss.

Somewhere between lunch and Runswick Bay, David must have filled his friend in on the events of the night before, and on Fliss's plan for that night. As he passed her seat on the coach, Gary bent down and whispered, 'OK – I'm in. Talk to you later.'

Clouds rolled in after tea, threatening rain. Team games on the beach were cancelled, and everybody went to their rooms to write up the day's activity. Each child was keeping a sort of log or diary of the visit, in which points of interest were to be recorded. Fliss wrote for a while, then got up and looked out of the window. The old woman was there watching the hotel. Fliss resolved to ask Mrs Wilkinson about her. She sat down again on her bunk, chewing the end of her pencil and reading through what she had written.

'Tuesday. Staithes and Runswick Bay. Nothing

happened on coach. Looked at scenery. Staithes old-fashioned and sort of dark with hills and cliffs all round. Mr Hepworth told us about the headless ghost but we didn't see it. We didn't see Captain Cook's shop either because it is under the sea. Crab pots everywhere. I had an ice-lolly and Mrs Marriott took our photo.'

'How d'you spell "excitement"?' asked Marie from her perch on the top bunk.

'Why – what're you writing about?'

'Mrs Evans. I'm putting, "There was a bit of excitement when we thought Mrs Evans had fallen off the cliff, but she'd only fallen behind, which was boring."'

'You're not.'

'I am.'

'I wouldn't be you, then. It's E-X-C-I-T-E-M-E-N-T.'

'Ta.'

Fliss knew she should write more, but she couldn't concentrate. If Lisa and the two boys were to watch with her tonight, they'd have to get together sometime this evening and sort out details, like where they'd meet and at what time.

She listened. Beyond the door, everything seemed quiet. Nobody was on the landing or the stairs. She wondered what the teachers were doing. If they were busy, she and Lisa might be able to slip down to the next floor and have a quick meeting with the boys. It was strictly forbidden to visit other people's rooms, but they'd have to risk it. She put her book and pencil on the bed and went to the door.

'Where you going?' asked Maureen.

'Toilet,' she lied, opening the door and looking out. The landing was deserted. She slipped out, closed the door and knocked on the door of room eleven.

'Who is it?' Samantha's voice.

'Fliss. Is Lisa there?'

'Yes. Just a minute.'

Voices beyond the door. Fliss glanced towards the cupboard. No number. Door eleven opened and Lisa looked out. 'Come on,' whispered Fliss.

'Where? I'm halfway through my log.'

'Trot's room. Make plans. Quiet.'

'OK.'

They tiptoed down the stairs, listening for teachers. There was nobody on the landing below. Doors seven and eight were closed.

'Which is theirs?' hissed Lisa.

'Seven. Watch the stairs while I knock.'

Lisa watched and listened. Fliss knocked.

'Who's there?' It sounded like Gary's voice.

'Fliss. Open up, quick.'

Footsteps approached the door. It opened a

crack. An eye peered out. 'On your own, are you?'

'Me and Lisa. Hurry up.'

The door opened. Gary and David came out. 'Aren't we using your room?' Fliss asked.

'No chance. Barry and Richard're in there. They know nothing about this. It'll have to be the bathroom.'

They slipped into the bathroom, and Gary pushed the door-catch into place. 'We'll have to make it quick,' he whispered. 'Somebody's bound to want the toilet before long, and anyway I haven't started my log yet.'

They made their plans swiftly. They would go to bed at nine as normal, and wait till their roommates fell asleep. That should be earlier than last night because they'd had a long, tiring walk. At twenty-five past eleven exactly they'd get out of bed. They wouldn't dress for fear of waking somebody. They would leave their rooms and meet in the top-floor bathroom, room twelve, at half-past eleven. From there they would be able to keep watch on the stair-top, landing and cupboard. It would be impossible for anyone to reach the cupboard without being seen, and if anything odd happened to the door itself, like the number thirteen suddenly appearing on it, they'd see that too.

This settled, the four split up and returned to their rooms. It wasn't until Fliss was lying in bed at half-past nine, listening to Marie and the twins, that she realized nobody had thought about what they'd do if Ellie-May did appear. She lay, worrying about this and looking at her watch every minute or two, as her room-mates chattered on.

It was nearly eleven o'clock before the girls in room ten stopped talking and three of them fell asleep. Fliss lay absolutely still, listening to their breathing, and almost drifted off herself. When she realized what was happening she shook her head, blinked rapidly and looked at her watch.

Twenty-three twenty. Ten minutes to zero. Now that it was nearly time she didn't fancy it one bit. The cold, dark landing. The door of the linen cupboard, upon which the number thirteen might at this very moment be materializing. The prospect of footfalls on the stair.

And I was the one who suggested it, she reminded herself. I must have been crazy.

Well, anyway, it was too late now. It was her plan and she was stuck with it. She squinted at her watch again. Twenty-three twenty-seven. Three minutes to zero. What she'd do was, she'd listen for the others arriving. One of the others, at least.

She didn't want to be the first. She knew that if she opened the door and found herself alone on the landing, just a metre or so from that creepy cupboard, she'd have the door shut and be back under the covers so quick her feet wouldn't touch the floor.

Listen. A creak somewhere. Somewhere a tick. The house, settling. Twenty-three twenty-nine, and no footsteps. Perhaps nobody'll turn up. Maybe they've fallen asleep. I nearly did. And if they have, it's off. There's no way I'm watching alone. No way. Please God, let them be asleep.

Zero hour, and listen – somebody's coming. Somebody's right outside the door, breathing. Waiting. And there – there goes a whisper, so there's two of them at least and they're whispering about me – asking where I am.

Asleep, that's where I am, so leave me. Let me sleep. There's three of you. You don't need me. You don't need me, do you? Do you?

Twenty-three thirty-one. Zero plus one. They're listening at the door, and they know you're not asleep. They can hear you breathing – looking at your watch. They can hear your heart.

My idea. My plan. My own stupid fault in other words. OK, OK. I'm coming. Here I come.

She got out of bed, tiptoed across the sandy carpet and stood with her ear to the door, listening to the sounds of stealthy movement beyond. Behind her, the three girls slept on. She twisted the knob and eased the door open. It squeaked, and somebody outside went, 'Sssh!' She looked across. Three pale figures were watching her from the bathroom doorway.

'Where the heck have you been?' hissed Lisa, as Fliss joined them. 'We've been here ages.'

'Sorry. I think I must have dropped off to sleep. Is anything happening?'

She looked towards the cupboard but there was no number. Trot shook his head. 'Nothing yet. Look, let's get inside and close the door except for a crack to look through. And no more talking, right?'

They stood on the cold plastic tiles, peering over one another's shoulders. The rain which had threatened earlier was now falling. Cloud hid the moon, so that the windows on the half-landings gave almost no light. Fliss shivered, wishing she had her dressing-gown and slippers, or better still, that she was where they were, in her bedroom at home.

Somewhere a clock chimed. 'What time's that?' whispered Gary. 'I forgot my flipping watch.'

Fliss looked at hers. 'Twenty-three forty-five – quarter to twelve.'

'Good grief, is that all? It feels like we've been

here for ever.' He withdrew from the doorway and walked up and down, hugging himself and shivering. Trot and Lisa drew back too, leaving Fliss to watch.

Nothing happened. After a while she said, 'Hey, how about somebody else taking a turn here? I need to get warm too.'

'I'll do it,' volunteered Lisa. Fliss went and stood on one leg beside the bath, resting a cold foot on its rim in order to massage some warmth into it. After a while she swapped over and rubbed the other foot.

Presently they heard the distant chimes again. Midnight. They looked at one another and drifted towards the door. As they did so, Lisa let out a stifled cry and pointed. 'Look.' They looked. The cupboard was room thirteen.

'Oh, wow,' moaned Gary. 'It's real. I thought it was a dream, but it's real.'

'You scared then?' Trot's words carried a challenge, but his voice came out a croak.

'I told you, didn't I?' breathed Fliss. 'I told you it wasn't a dream.'

'Oh, Fliss,' whimpered Lisa. 'Oh, my God, what am I doing here?' Fliss put an arm round her friend and squeezed. 'It's OK, Lisa. Take it easy. It's just a door with a number on it, right? We don't have to go in there or anything. We don't even have to go near it, for goodness sake.' She looked at the others. 'What now?'

'Listen!' Trot was watching the stairs. 'I think someone's coming.'

'Oh, no!' Gary crammed all of his fingers in his mouth and stood, gazing at the stair-top and shaking his head.

There came the unmistakable sound of footfalls slowly ascending, and a pale shape came into view. Trot grabbed Fliss's arm. 'It's Ellie-May.'

'Sssh!'

'But shouldn't we try to stop her? Look where she's going for heaven's sake.'

'No!' Fliss shook her head. 'She's asleep, I think – sleepwalking, and you're not supposed to wake sleepwalkers. We'll watch what happens and tell the teachers in the morning.'

Lisa looked at her. 'That was part of the plan, was it?'

'Yes.' It wasn't, of course. She hadn't even considered what they might do if events reached this stage. She only knew she couldn't leave this bathroom right now to save her life. Hers, or anybody else's.

They watched. Ellie-May crossed the landing to the cupboard door and reached for the knob. She hesitated for a moment with her hand on it, then twisted and pushed. The watchers peered intently

77

as the door swung inward, but from where they were they couldn't see anything beyond it except darkness. They watched Ellie-May walk into that darkness and close the door.

'Phew!' Gary moved from the door again, shaking his head. 'I don't get it, Trot. What does she do in there?'

The other boy shrugged. 'I don't know, do I?'

'Does anybody fancy having a look?' whispered Lisa.

Gary looked at her. 'Do you?' She shook her head.

'I think we should wait here till she comes out,' said Fliss.

They waited. Half-past twelve came, and a quarter to one. They didn't take turns now but huddled together, watching the door through eyes that burned, while their feet grew numb. From time to time, faint sounds reached them from beyond the door: sounds which might have made them shiver, even if they had not been cold. It was almost a quarter-past one when the noises ceased, and a few minutes after that when the door opened and Ellie-May reappeared. They watched as she closed the door, crossed the landing and slipped away down the stairs.

'Well,' breathed Gary, 'what now?'

'I vote we go get old Hepworth,' said Trot, 'and

let him have a look in that cupboard.'

'No.' Fliss shook her head. 'What if Ellie-May wasn't sleepwalking at all? What if she's been up to something in there – something she shouldn't? We don't know, do we? If we fetch Mr Hepworth we could land her in serious trouble.'

Lisa gazed at her friend. 'Ellie-May's always getting other kids in trouble,' she said. 'I don't think we should worry too much about that.'

Gary nodded. 'I'm with Lisa,' he said.

'Me too,' growled Trot. 'There's something weird going on here, Fliss. We can't keep it to ourselves. Not when Ellie-May might be in danger.'

Fliss nodded. 'OK. I wasn't suggesting we keep it to ourselves indefinitely – just till morning. I'll have a word with Ellie-May before breakfast. Tell her we saw her. Ask her what she was doing. Then, if she doesn't come up with a satisfactory explanation we bring in the teachers. How's that?'

Gary shrugged. 'Sounds fair enough to me. Give her a chance to explain.'

'All right,' said Lisa.

'OK,' sighed Trot. 'I'm too shattered to argue anyway.'

They left the bathroom and tiptoed away to their beds, but dawn was breaking over the sea before any one of them slept.

16

'Fliss – hey, Fliss!' Somebody was shaking her roughly. She opened her eyes to find Marie grinning down at her. 'Come on, lazybones – you're going to be late for breakfast and it's the abbey today.'

'Mmm.' She pulled up the covers and turned her head away. 'Leave me here,' she mumbled. 'I just want to sleep for ever.'

'You'll write apologies for ever if you make us late. Everybody else has finished in the bathroom and some have gone downstairs.'

Bathroom. Last night. Something she said she'd do. 'Oh, crikey!' She threw back the covers, leapt out of bed and grabbed her towel. 'Listen, Marie – will you do me a favour?'

'What?'

'Make my bed while I get washed? I'm supposed to see Ellie-May. I wanted to catch her before she went downstairs. Please?'

'OK.' Marie smiled. 'Just this once. Go on.'

Fliss ran across the landing, forgetting in her haste to check the linen cupboard door. She washed rapidly, splashing a lot of water about. It doesn't seem two minutes since I was in here before, she thought.

When she returned to room ten her bed was neatly made and Marie had gone. She pulled on some clothes, dragged a comb through her hair and headed for the stairs. Five past eight. Breakfast was at eight o'clock. Ellie-May would be in the dining-room by now, with no empty place at her table, and Lisa and the boys would be cursing her for being last again.

The third-floor landing was deserted, which meant that Trot and Gary had gone down. The next floor was Ellie-May's. Fliss ran down the stairs and nearly bumped into Mrs Evans and Mr Hepworth, who were talking in the doorway of room four. She slowed down and tried to creep past, but Mrs Evans said, 'Stop, Felicity Morgan. Come here.'

'Yes, Miss?'

'Yes, Miss? I'll give you "yes, Miss". What time do you call this?'

'Five past eight, Miss.'

'Nearly six minutes past, actually. And what time's breakfast?'

'Eight o'clock, Miss.'

'Exactly. So you're six minutes late. And you were running. Why were you running, Felicity?'

''Cause I'm six minutes late, Miss.'

'Don't be cheeky! You've broken two rules already. Mrs Marriott will be in the dining-room. Tell her Ellie-May's not well, and that Mr Hepworth and I will be down in a minute. Have you got that?'

'Yes, Miss.'

'Off you go then. And think on – I'll be watching you, Felicity.'

She hurried on down. She didn't run, but her mind was racing. Ellie-May's not well and there are two teachers outside her room. She's in bed, then. That means I won't get to talk to her, so what do we do – keep quiet about last night, or tell the teachers? Tell, I suppose.

Everybody was eating cornflakes. Trot gave her a dirty look as she walked in. Mrs Marriott was sitting alone at the teachers' table, chewing watchfully.

Fliss delivered her message, and was sent down to the kitchen to apologize to Mrs Wilkinson for being late, and to ask if she might have some cornflakes. As the woman shook cereal into a bowl for her, Fliss said, 'There's an old lady sits in the shelter across the road.

82

She seems to be there all the time. Who is she?'

Mrs Wilkinson smiled, pouring milk. 'You must mean old Sal,' she said. 'Sally Haggerlythe. She's mad, I'm afraid. Got some sort of bee in her bonnet about this place – mumbles on about fate and doom and dread and I don't know what. I'd steer clear of old Sal if I were you.'

Fliss said nothing, but thought it might be interesting sometime to have a word with mad Sal Haggerlythe.

She carried her cereal bowl to the dining-room and slipped into the only empty place. None of the other three was at her table, but two tables away sat Gary, facing her. He was looking at her with an expression which was angry and questioning at the same time.

She began mouthing at him, voicelessly, exaggerating her lip-movements and pointing to the ceiling. She's in bed, she mouthed. Sick. I didn't get to talk to her. She spread her hands, palms upward, and shrugged. What do we do?

Gary might have been good at all sorts of things, but lip-reading wasn't one of them. He glared at Fliss, scowling and shaking his head. She began again, even more slowly, stretching her lips and jabbing at the ceiling, then bent forward, goggle-eyed, clutching her throat and shooting out her tongue as if puking into her bowl.

'What on earth's the matter with you, Felicity Morgan?' Mrs Marriott was looking at her as though at a lunatic.

'She's lost her marbles, Miss,' said Gary, and some of the kids sniggered.

'Nobody asked you, Gary Bazzard. Well, Felicity?'

'I had a bit of cornflake stuck in my throat, Miss. It's gone now.'

'I'm glad about that,' said the teacher, acidly, 'because, you see, the rest of us have finished our cornflakes and Mr Wilkinson is waiting to clear, so that Mrs Wilkinson can serve sausages and bacon before they go cold.'

'Yes, Miss.'

She spooned cereal into her mouth and chewed, keeping her head down. Everybody was looking at her. She could feel their eyes. She ate distractedly, thinking about mad Sal and the whispering voice of her dream. It seemed like hours before her bowl was empty.

When everybody had finished breakfast, Mrs Evans stood up and said, 'Now – I want you all to go back to your rooms and get ready for our walk. We're running a bit late, so you haven't got long. I'd like everybody in the lounge, kitted up and ready to go, by nine o'clock. What time did I say, Felicity Morgan?'

'Nine o'clock, Miss.'

'Right. Table one, off you go.'

Felicity's was the last table to be dismissed, but the others were waiting for her outside Gary and Trot's room on the third landing.

'What was that pantomime you were putting on for me down there?' demanded Gary. 'I couldn't make head nor tail of it.' He was holding the giant stick of rock, which he'd sucked almost to a point at one end. He sucked it now as he gazed at Fliss. She shuddered.

'I don't know how you can,' she said, 'straight after breakfast. Mrs Evans and old Hepworth were by Ellie-May's door when I came down, so I didn't get to see her. That's what I was trying to tell you.'

'The point is, what do we do?' said Lisa.

Trot looked at Fliss. 'There's nobody by Ellie-May's door now, is there? The teachers are all downstairs. You could go and talk to her, like you were going to.'

Fliss shook her head. 'The other kids're there. She wouldn't tell me anything in front of them, would she?'

'I reckon we'll just have to tell about last night,' said Gary. 'She was poorly yesterday, and now she's worse. Who knows what might happen if we keep it to ourselves? I think you should go to Mr Hepworth, Fliss.'

'Why me?'

Gary grinned. 'He'd never believe me, nobody does, but he'll believe you. And anyway, the whole thing was your idea, wasn't it – keeping watch and that?'

'All right.' Fliss nodded. 'But I still wish we could have talked to Ellie-May first.'

She found Mr Hepworth in the downstairs hallway, handing out packed lunches. There was a queue. Fliss tagged on the end. When she got to the front she took the little packet he offered and said, 'Sir, can I have a word? It's about Ellie-May.'

'What about Ellie-May?' Kids were waiting in line behind her and he was anxious to give out the rest of the lunches.

'It's about what's wrong with her, Sir.'

'And what's that to do with you, Felicity?'

'Sir, I think I know why she's ill.'

'Indeed? It's Doctor Morgan now, is it? Go on then – why is Ellie-May ill?'

'She goes in the cupboard on the top floor, Sir. At night. I heard her on Monday night, and David Trotter saw her. And last night four of us kept watch and she went in again.'

Mr Hepworth looked at her. 'Are you trying to

wind me up, Felicity Morgan? Ellie-May Sunderland's a sensible girl. Why on earth would she be creeping about in the middle of the night, getting into cupboards? I never heard anything so daft in my life.' He smiled thinly. 'Just as a matter of interest, who were the three who kept this watch with you?'

'Lisa Watmough, Sir, And David Trotter and Gary Bazzard.'

'Ah! I thought Gary Bazzard's name might crop up. He put you up to this, didn't he?'

'No, Sir. We saw her, Sir, honestly. There was a thirteen on the door and it's not there in the daytime.'

The teacher's lips twitched. 'And somebody lives in the cupboard, right? Now let me guess who that might be.' He looked at the ceiling for a moment, then slapped his hands together. 'I know – it's Dracula, isn't it?'

Fliss gazed at him, appalled. 'D'you – d'you think it could be, Sir?'

Mr Hepworth looked at her. The smile faded from his eyes. 'Good heavens, Felicity, I do believe you're serious. Somebody's frightened you half to death, haven't they? Now who's been telling you stories, eh? Gary Bazzard, was it?'

'No, Sir. It's not a story, Sir. Honestly. Will you have a look in the cupboard?'

87

The teacher sighed, gazing at her now with sympathetic eyes. 'All right, Felicity. I'll have a look, and you'd better look too. A cupboard's just a cupboard, as you'll see.' He looked along the line of waiting children. 'Waseem – come and give out the rest of these lunches, will you?'

'Sir.'

Together they climbed to the top of the house and crossed the landing. Fliss hung back as Mr Hepworth twisted the doorknob and pulled. Nothing happened. 'It's locked,' he said.

'You pulled, Sir,' said Fliss. 'Try pushing.'

'There's no point, Felicity – it opens outwards.'

'Ellie-May pushed it last night, Sir.'

'But that's impossible, Felicity. It's made to open outwards – you can tell by the hinges.'

'Get the key, Sir – please.'

He sighed. 'If it's locked now, it must have been locked last night. I think you had a nightmare, Felicity. You dreamed you were watching, but you were asleep. Dreams can seem very real sometimes, but if it'll set your mind at rest I'll go and ask Mrs Wilkinson for the key. Wait here.'

She waited till he turned on the half-landing and passed from sight, then followed quickly, seizing her chance.

The door of room four was closed. Fliss twisted the knob and pushed gently, praying that neither

Mrs Evans nor Mrs Marriott would be in the room.

They weren't. The room, like her own, contained a double bed and a pair of bunks. Ellie-May was in the bottom bunk. She lay on her back with her eyes closed. Her face was almost as white as the pillow. Fliss knelt down and touched her shoulder.

'Ellie-May. Are you awake? It's Fliss.'

Ellie-May's eyelids fluttered. She rolled her head towards Fliss and mumbled, 'What? Oh, it's you. I thought everybody'd gone out. What d'you want?'

'I want you to tell me what happens in that cupboard, Ellie-May. I want you to tell Mr Hepworth too.'

Ellie-May's brow puckered. 'Cupboard?'

'On the top floor. You went there last night. We saw you.'

'No.' She shook her head. 'Nowhere last night. Here. Not very well. Flu, Mrs Evans says. Tablets make me sleepy. Give me dreams.'

'What sort of dreams?' she tightened her grip on the other girl's shoulder. 'What sort of dreams, Ellie-May?'

Ellie-May grimaced. 'Horrible dreams. Dark house. Empty, I think. Stairs. Lots of stairs, and a room. The room of – oh, I forget. Why don't you bog off and leave me alone? I'm off to sleep.'

She rolled her head towards the wall, and the movement exposed the side of her neck. Fliss's eyes widened and she almost cried out. In the pale skin under Ellie-May's ear were two spots of dried blood.

As she stared at the marks on the sick girl's neck, Fliss heard footfalls on the stair. Mr Hepworth was on his way up with the key. She didn't know whether to rush out and drag him in now, or wait till he'd seen inside the cupboard. The cupboard, she decided. Once he'd had a look in there he surely wouldn't need any dragging.

She waited till he'd passed by, then left the room and followed him up. When she reached the top landing he was there, dangling a key on a piece of thick string. He said, 'Where've you been? I told you to wait here.'

'I had to go to the bathroom, Sir. I was scared to use this one.'

He looked at her and shook his head. 'Silly girl. Now watch.'

He inserted the key in the lock, twisted it and pulled. The door opened. Fliss saw darkness and hung back. The teacher beckoned. 'Come along,

Felicity – you're the one who thought we should look inside.' She moved forward and looked.

It was just a cupboard. A walk-in cupboard with a narrow gangway between tiers of shelving. Stacked neatly on the shelves were sheets, pillow-cases and towels. Two metres from the threshold, the gangway ended in a blank wall. There was nothing else.

'There you are, you see.' Mr Hepworth closed and re-locked the door. 'No bats, no monsters and no number thirteen. Does that make you feel better?'

Fliss shook her head. 'It's different at night, Sir. It changes. Could you keep the key and look tonight?'

'Certainly not!' He gave her an angry look. 'Now see here, Felicity – this nonsense has gone quite far enough. You asked me to come up here. I was busy, but I came. You asked me to fetch the key. I did. You've seen for yourself that this is just an ordinary cupboard. Either you had a nightmare in which it became something else, or this whole thing has been a silly prank dreamed up by Gary Bazzard. Either way, it stops right here. D'you understand?'

Fliss nodded, looking at the floor. There was an aching lump in her throat and she had to bite her lip to keep from crying. What about Ellie-May?

Those marks. What would he do if she mentioned them now? Go out of his tree, probably. Yet she must tell him. She must.

'Sir?'

'What is it now?' He was striding towards the stairs.

She trotted at his heels. 'Ellie-May's got blood on her neck, Sir. Dried blood.'

They began descending, rapidly. Without looking at her he said, 'Rubbish, Felicity Morgan! Absolute rubbish. One more word out of you, and you'll find yourself writing lines this evening while everybody else goes swimming. Right?'

Right. Miserably, she followed him down. Everybody was out on the pavement, waiting for them, hacking at the flagstones with the toes of their strong boots and scowling into the hallway. All except Ellie-May.

Hallway – Ellie-May – Bed – Dread.

Dead.

They walked through the old town, up the one hundred and ninety-nine steps and across the graveyard to the abbey. They were in their groups, so Fliss didn't get to talk to Lisa who, with Trot, was in Mrs Marriott's group. She talked to Gary, who these days always smelled of peppermint. She told him how she'd seen inside the cupboard, and that it was just a cupboard. She told him how sick Ellie-May looked, and about the blood on her neck. When she told him about the blood, his cheeks went pale and he whispered, 'Crikey – are you sure, Fliss?' She assured him she was, absolutely sure.

He told her he'd overheard Mrs Evans and Mr Hepworth talking. Mrs Wilkinson had been there too. They were discussing Ellie-May. Mrs Evans said she thought they should phone Ellie-May's parents. Mr Hepworth was in favour of waiting another day – it was probably just a touch of flu, he said. Mrs Wilkinson mentioned homesickness and the change of water. It happened all the time, she assured them. Children were in and out of The Crow's Nest every week between Easter and October, and in nearly every group there was one child who grew pale and listless and lost its appetite through homesickness and the change of water.

'I didn't hear the end of it,' said Gary, 'but I think they decided to wait till tomorrow.'

Fliss scowled. 'Grown-ups are so stupid,' she muttered. 'They never believe anything you tell them. If Ellie-May goes in that cupboard again tonight it might be too late to call her parents.'

'What're we going to do? Shall I have a go at talking to old Hepworth?'

'No. I told you – he thinks the whole thing's a tale and that it was you who made it up.'

'Yeah,' sighed Gary. 'He would. I always get the blame for everything. It's the same at home.'

'When we're looking round the abbey,' said Fliss, 'they won't keep us in our groups. Let's talk to Trot and Lisa – see what they think.'

There wasn't much left of the abbey – just some crumbling sections of wall, very high in places, with tidy lawns between. There were a lot of sightseers though, including other school groups, and it was easy for Fliss and the other three to get together behind a chunk of ancient masonry and talk. Fliss told Trot and Lisa her story, and they tossed ideas back and forth. In the end it came to this. None of the teachers would believe them, so they were on their own. They were all agreed that Ellie-May must not be allowed to enter the cupboard again, so they'd watch and if she came they'd stop her, by force if necessary.

'Right,' said Fliss. 'That's settled. Now, d'you think we can forget about Ellie-May and that ghastly cupboard, just for a few hours, and have some fun? We're supposed to be on holiday, you know.'

Gary pulled a wry face. 'It won't be easy, Fliss.'

Trot shrugged. 'I'm scared as a rat thinking about tonight, but what's the point? Fretting isn't going to make it go away, so we might as well enjoy ourselves while we can.'

'Trot's right,' said Lisa. 'We're on holiday. Let's at least explore some of these ruins before the teachers get bored and call us together.'

They split up and wandered about, gazing at the walls and the high, slender windows. Fliss tried to imagine what the place must have looked like long ago, with a roof, and stained glass, and flagstones where all this grass now grew, but it was impossible. Anyway, she told herself, I like it better as it is now. You can see the sky. There are birds,

and grass, and sunlight, and I don't like gloomy
places.

She shivered.

They stayed an hour among the ruins, then assembled for the clifftop walk to Saltwick Bay. It was just after eleven o'clock. The sun, which had shone brightly as they left The Crow's Nest, was now a fuzzy pink ball. A cool breeze was coming off the sea, and the eastern horizon was hidden by mist.

Mr Hepworth gazed out to sea. 'This mist is known as a sea-fret,' he told them, 'and sea-frets are very common on this coast. You probably feel a bit chilled just now, but once we start walking you'll be all right.' He turned and pointed. 'That collection of buildings is the Coastguard Station. The path goes right past it, and that's where this morning's walk really begins. Who can tell us what coastguards do? Yes, Keith?'

'Guard the coast, Sir.'

'Well, yes. What sort of things do they look out for, d'you think?'

'Shipwrecks, Sir. People drowning and that.'

'That's right. Vessels or persons in trouble at sea – including those silly beggars who keep getting themselves washed out on lilos and old tyres. They also watch for people stuck or injured on cliffs, and for distress rockets and signs of foul weather. Right – let's go.'

They filed across the Abbey Plain and up past the Coastguard Station. The path was part of the Cleveland Way, and countless boots had churned it into sticky mud, permanent except in the longest dry spells. Because of this, duckboards had been laid down, so that most of the path between Whitby and Saltwick was under wooden slats.

'What a weird track,' said Maureen. 'It's like a raft that goes on for ever.'

'I hope it doesn't go on for ever,' her twin retorted. 'It kills your feet.'

It didn't go on for ever. They'd been walking twenty-five minutes, on the flat and over stiles, when the boards ended and they found themselves on a tarmac road which went through the middle of a caravan holiday camp. Just beyond the camp was a muddy pathway which led from the clifftop to the beach. Mr Hepworth lifted his hand.

'Right. This is Saltwick Bay.' He looked at his watch. 'It's twenty-five to twelve, and if it stays fine we'll be here till about half-past four, so there's plenty of time. We'll eat lunch at half-past twelve. In the meantime you may paddle, play on the sand, look for fossils in the cliff-face or collect shells and pebbles on the beach. You are not, repeat not, to do any of the following: sit down in the surf and get your clothing wet. Attempt to climb the cliff. Throw stones or other hard missiles. Murder one another. Chuck your best friend into the sea. Utter shrieks, bellows or similar prehistoric noises, or find a tiny child with a sandcastle and flatten the sandcastle, the tiny child, or both. Is that clear?'

It was.

The bay was sandy in some parts and rocky in others. Fliss and Lisa sat on a rock to remove their boots and socks, then ran down to the water's edge, where they rolled up their jeans and waited for a wavelet to wash over their feet.

'Ooh, it's freezing!' Fliss scampered clear and stood with her hands in her anorak pockets, curling her toes in the wet sand. Lisa gasped and screwed up her face but refused to budge. The wavelet spent itself and rushed back.

'Hey, that's weird!' She flung out her arms for balance. 'If you look down when the wave's going back you seem to be sliding backwards up the beach at terrific speed – like skiing in reverse. I nearly fell over.'

'I remember that from when I was little,' said

Fliss. 'It happened the first time I ever paddled. I howled, and it was ages before my mum could get me in the sea again.'

'There's something else as well,' laughed Lisa, as a second wavelet ran back. 'The water washes the sand away from under your heels. It's like a big hole opening up to swallow you. I bet that's why you were frightened. Come and have a go.'

They played along the edge of the sea till it was half-past twelve and Mrs Evans called them to come and eat lunch. They sat on rocks and munched, burying their feet in the dry sand for warmth.

'I'd no idea it was lunchtime,' said Fliss. 'We only seem to have been here about five minutes.'

'That's 'cause we're having fun,' Lisa replied. 'If it was maths, it'd seem like five hours.'

Grant Cooper and Robert Field had been looking for fossils along the foot of the cliff. They'd dug some out and brought them back in a polythene bag. Mr Hepworth tipped them on a flat rock and spread them out. Everybody gathered round, and the teacher picked out the best specimens.

'Look at this.' He held up a slender, cylindrical object which came to a point at one end. 'This is a belemnite. It lived in the sea millions of years ago and looked something like a squid.'

'It looks something like a bullet now,' observed Andrew Roberts. Mrs Evans gave him one of her looks.

'And this one's a gryphia, or devil's toenail, to give it its popular name. It looks similar to a mussel, but it too lived millions of years ago. And this,' he held up a thick disc with a curled pattern on it, 'is an ammonite. It looks snail-like, and you might think it slithered slowly along the seabed but it didn't. It swam, catching its food with its many tentacles.'

'How do they know, Sir?' asked Haley Denton.

'Know what, Haley?'

'That it swam about, Sir. There were no people then, and there are no ammerites or whatever now, so how do they know what it did?'

'Ah – good question, Haley. Well, one thing they do is look at creatures which are built in a similar way, and are alive today. There's a creature called the nautilus which is something like an ammonite. They know how it gets around, so they're pretty sure the ammonite got around in a similar way. D'you see?'

'Yes, Sir.'

When everything had been eaten and washed down with canned pop, the children went off in twos and threes to do whatever they felt like doing. It was a quarter-past one. The mist had thickened, blotting out the sun, and the breeze gusted spitefully, sharp with blown sand. The holidaymakers had withdrawn to their caravans, so that the children of Bottomtop Middle had the beach to themselves. They went barefoot, but did not remove their anoraks.

Fliss and Lisa ranged far along the tideline, looking for shells and fancy pebbles. They found no shells, except some blue-black fragments of broken mussel which they spurned. There were plenty of pebbles though, and some were quite pretty, especially when wet. They picked up the best ones, putting them in the bags they'd saved from lunch. It was absorbing work, and when Fliss finally looked up she was amazed to see how far they'd come.

'Hey, look – we're miles from anyone else. The teachers look like dots.'

'That's just how I like them,' chuckled Lisa. 'We can't go any further, though – we've run out of beach.'

It was true. In front of them a great, dark headland jutted into the sea. Gulls skimmed screaming along the face of its cliff but the still air felt less cold.

'There's no wind here,' said Fliss. 'Let's stay for a bit. Look – the tide's swept all the rubbish into a corner like Mrs Clarke at school. There might be something good.'

They waded through the flotsam with their heads down, turning it over with their feet, exclaiming from time to time as some new find came to light. A lobster pot smashed in a storm. A clump of orange line, hopelessly tangled. A dead gull.

Fliss worked steadily along the base of the cliff, seeking mermaids and Spanish gold. She heard the hiss of surf on sand, and glanced up to find she'd almost reached the sea. As she stood looking out, her eyes were drawn to a dark, spray-drenched rock, and to the bird which sat on it.

It was black, and it held out its ragged wings as though waiting for the wind to dry them. Fliss shivered as she gazed at it, feeling the magic drain out of the day. It reminded her of something. A witch perhaps, or a broken umbrella. Or the iron crow on the Gate of Fate.

When Fliss and Lisa got back, the teachers had already called everybody together for the return journey. It was only a quarter-past three, but the mist had thickened and there was a hint of drizzle in it. Some of the kids were sitting on rocks, drying their feet with gritty towels, pulling on socks and boots. Others stood waiting with their hoods up and bags of pebbles dangling at their sides. A small party, supervised by Mrs Evans, was picking up the last scraps of litter. Bottomtop Middle prided itself on the fact that whenever a group of its children vacated a site, they left no evidence that they had ever been there.

As they trudged up towards the path in the cliff, Fliss saw a large, slate-coloured pebble lying on the sand. Something about it appealed to her — its perfect oval shape perhaps, or its wonderful smoothness. She bent and picked it up. It was thick, and far heavier than she'd expected, and when she tried to add it to the collection in her polythene bag, it wouldn't fit. She was cramming it in her anorak pocket when Mrs Evans, who was bringing up the rear, said, 'Felicity – you don't really want that, dear. It's far too big. You'll be crippled by the time you've carried it all the way back to Whitby, not to mention the fact that it'll probably tear your pocket. Throw it away.'

Fliss was a quiet girl who never argued with her teachers, and so she surprised herself as well as Mrs Evans when she said, 'I like it, Miss. I want to keep it.'

It was lucky for Fliss that Richard Varley chose that moment to leap on Barry Tune's back. As the two boys fell on to the sand, Mrs Evans called sharply and hurried to separate them, and by the time she had done so the line of children was toiling up the cliff path. She had to put on a spurt to catch up, and the pebble incident was forgotten.

The rest of the walk back was uneventful, except that it started to rain in earnest which made the duckboards slippery. Several children fell, to the delight of the rest, who laughed and cheered their classmates' misfortune.

By twenty to five they were back at The Crow's Nest, drenched and happy. They were sent to their rooms to change and to write up their journals. It was during this interlude that Fliss and Lisa, Trot and Gary met briefly on the fourth-floor landing.

'We all set for tonight?' asked Fliss. She felt tense, and was amazed that for a few hours today she'd actually succeeded in forgetting about all of this.

The others nodded. 'Same time, same place,' said Trot. 'And let's hope nothing happens.'

'Any news of Ellie-May?' asked Lisa.

Gary shrugged. 'I saw Mrs Marriott going into her room as I came up. Maybe they'll call her parents to take her home or something.'

'Oh, I wish they would,' sighed Fliss. 'I'm fed up of feeling scared.'

Trot nodded. 'Me too.'

'We all are,' said Lisa. 'Who wouldn't be?'

After tea, everybody had to rest quietly for an hour in their rooms to let their food settle before Mrs Evans took them swimming. Fliss couldn't rest. There was something she had to do. She looked out of the window. Yes, old Sal was there as usual. Mumbling something about going to the toilet, Fliss left the room, slipped down the stairs and let herself out. It was still raining.

The old woman looked up as the girl reached the shelter. Fliss smiled. 'Hello.'

Sal nodded. 'Evenin'.'

Fliss blushed, looking down at her feet. She didn't know what to say.

'I – I'm staying at The Crow's Nest.'

'Aye, I know.'

'I've seen you lots of times. Through the window.'

The crone nodded. 'Windows is the eyes of a house.'

Fliss smiled. 'Yes. Eyes, watching the sea. Lucky old house.'

'Lucky?' Something rattled in Sal's throat. 'You're wrong, child. It's got the other eye, see. The eye that sleeps by day.'

'Oh, has it?' Fliss smiled, not sure whether she ought to. The eye that sleeps by day. Sounds barmy but then, so does room thirteen. Should she mention room thirteen to Sal? No. There wasn't time. It only needed a teacher to look in room ten and she'd be in more trouble. She looked at the old woman. 'I'd better get back. They'll be wondering –' She let the sentence hang, turned and ran through the rain with her head down.

Nobody had missed her, and when the swimming party set out twenty minutes later old Sal had gone. The rain-lashed streets were practically deserted, and when they got to the pool they found that they had it almost to themselves. They made the most of it, leaping and splashing and whooping in the warm, clear water under Mrs Evans' watchful gaze. A puzzled frown settled for a moment on the teacher's face when she noticed four of the children standing by the steps at the shallow end, taking no part in the revelry. Odd, she mused. Very odd. You'd think they were non-swimmers or something, but they're not. Still, it's up to them, isn't it? Perhaps they're tired from the walk today. Her eyes moved on, and the frown dissolved.

**21**

Nobody called Ellie-May's parents, or took her home. The word was that she was a little better, and might even be with them on the coach to Robin Hood's Bay the following day.

Fliss wasn't fooled. At ten o'clock she was lying on her back, staring at the wire mesh under Marie's mattress, waiting for half-past eleven. Her hands were folded across her chest, and under them was the pebble from Saltwick Bay. She felt its weight when she breathed, and her fingers caressed its perfect, soothing smoothness.

She was tired. Not from swimming – neither she nor the other three had swum – but from the exertions of the day and a sleepless night before. The swimming must have finished off Marie and the twins, because they were zonked out already. She listened to their breathing and wondered if she could stay awake.

She didn't. Not completely. At least twice she

drifted off and woke with a start, thinking she'd missed the witching hour, but there was to be no such luck. When the town clock chimed for eleven-thirty she was wide awake, and scared.

This time she got to the bathroom first. Trot and Gary came nearly straightaway, but it was nineteen minutes to twelve when the door of room eleven opened and Lisa slipped out.

'Sorry I'm late,' she whispered. 'I fell asleep.'

'It's OK,' Fliss told her. 'I fell asleep too – twice.'

'I was spark-out,' admitted Trot. 'This div had to shake me like a madman to wake me up.' He looked at Gary. 'Didn't you, Gaz?'

Gary nodded. 'You should've got yourself a stick of rock like mine. I sucked that from ten o'clock and didn't nod off once.'

'Dirty pig!' shuddered Lisa. 'I don't know how you can.'

Gary grinned. 'You should see it – it's getting a really good point on it now.'

'Tell you what I do want to see tonight,' said Fliss. 'I want to see how the thirteen gets on that door. I want to be watching when the clock starts striking midnight – see the exact moment the number appears.'

'Yeah.' Trot nodded. 'Good idea. Let's do that.'

'I've brought my torch,' said Lisa. 'We can shine

it on the door – right where the number will be. We'll see really clearly then.'

They waited. Gary, sitting on the rim of the bath, looked at his watch every few seconds. Fliss went to the hand basin, ran a trickle of cold water into her cupped hand and sucked it up, watching herself in the mirror. Trot stood by the window, gazing out. The patterned glass splintered the light from a streetlamp. Lisa leaned on the wall by the door, switching her torch on and off.

After a while Fliss whispered, 'Maybe she won't come.'

'It's only five to,' Gary told her. 'Plenty of time yet.' He hoped Fliss was right.

When his watch told him it was a minute to midnight, Gary got up and went over to the door. The others joined him, jostling quietly till they could all see and Lisa was at the front with her torch. 'Thirteen seconds,' he hissed, and began counting down. At fifteen seconds Lisa switched on and steadied the disc of light on the right spot.

It was not spectacular. As Gary whispered, 'Zero,' they heard the town clock chime, then strike. At about the fourth stroke they noticed a small shapeless mark on the door, and Lisa moved the torch slightly to get it in the centre of her beam. It was like a stain, lighter than the surrounding woodwork. As stroke followed stroke, the stain seemed to shrink and become paler, and then to divide, becoming two whitish blobs whose shapes altered until, by the twelfth stroke, they formed the figures one and three. As the echo died, they heard a door close somewhere below.

'I think she's coming,' warned Fliss. 'Switch the torch off, Lisa.' She did so, plunging the landing into darkness. They withdrew and half closed the door again.

'Did you see that?' breathed Trot. 'It just came out of nowhere. I can't believe it.'

Fliss snorted. 'You've got to believe it, you div – you saw it. The point is, what do we do when Ellie-May gets here?'

'We stop her,' hissed Gary. 'By force if we have to. We agreed.'

'OK, but which of us actually goes out there and grabs her – or do we all go?'

Lisa shook her head. 'We can't all go. It'd scare her to death. It should be a girl, Fliss – you or me. But I think we should try calling her first – from here.'

'Sssh!' Trot pressed a finger to his lips. 'She's here.'

They looked out. Ellie-May was standing on the top step, looking at the door to room thirteen. She hesitated for a moment, then moved forward. Lisa nudged Fliss. 'You, or me?'

'Me.' As Ellie-May drew level with the bath-room, Fliss cupped her mouth with her hands and hissed, 'Ellie-May!'

The girl didn't turn or pause, but continued walking slowly towards the cupboard. Using her full voice this time, Fliss called out, 'Ellie-May – over here!'

It made no difference. The girl was standing before the door now, reaching for the knob. Fliss felt a push in the small of her back and Lisa hissed, 'Go on, for heaven's sake – before she opens that door!'

She left the bathroom and moved across the landing, approaching Ellie-May from the rear. As the girl's hand closed round the knob, Fliss took a gentle grip on her shoulder and said, 'Ellie-May – You don't want to go in there.'

She felt the thin shoulder stiffen under her hand. Ellie-May's head turned, slowly, and Fliss found herself gazing into eyes which were dead as a shark's. The girl's lips twitched. 'Let go of me,' she hissed. 'Leave me alone.'

'Ellie-May!' Fliss swung her round and held her by both shoulders. 'Listen. We're trying to help you. If you go in that room, you'll die!'

Ellie-May snarled, shaking her head. 'Never die. Never. You, not me.' She tore herself from Fliss's grip and turned, scrabbling for the doorknob.

'Gary!' cried Fliss. 'Lisa. Quick – I can't hold her!' There was a scampering of bare feet on carpet and they were with her, the three of them. Hands reached out, snatching fistfuls of Ellie-May's clothing, circling her wrists. She hissed and fought, amazingly strong, freeing one hand to twist the doorknob and push.

The door swung inward. Fliss, one arm crooked round Ellie-May's neck, glanced inside and saw not a cupboard, but the room of her dream. There was the table with the long, pale box upon it and beyond, a small, curtained window. A window which wasn't there in the daytime. The eye that sleeps by day! She dug her heels into the carpet, threw her weight backwards and fell with Ellie-May on top of her.

'Quick, one of you – close that door!' She flung both arms round Ellie-May's waist and held on as the girl bucked and writhed. Lisa dropped to her knees, grabbed Ellie-May's legs and fell forward, pinning them under her. Fliss heard the door slam, and then the boys were there, catching the girl's wildly flailing arms. Ellie-May fought on for a moment but they were too many for her. Fliss felt the thin body go limp, and the girl began to cry. When they let go of her she lay curled on her side with a thumb in her mouth, moaning softly.

They got up and stood, looking down at her. 'What do we do now?' asked Lisa.

As she spoke, they heard voices below and footsteps on the stair. 'It won't be up to us,' said Gary. 'Here comes the cavalry.'

22

'What on earth's going on here?' The landing light came on, and there stood Mrs Evans, unfamiliar in a quilted dressing-gown and no make-up. She saw Ellie-May on the floor and hurried forward, dropping on one knee beside her.

'She was – we were –' Fliss floundered, seeking words which might make their story credible, while the teacher lifted Ellie-May's head on to her lap and checked with hands and eyes for damage. Mrs Marriott appeared in a beige nightie, followed closely by Mr Hepworth in maroon pyjamas. The door of room ten opened and Marie's sleepy face peered out.

'Marie Nero!' snapped Mr Hepworth. 'Get back into bed – now!' The door closed. He looked at Ellie-May, sobbing in Mrs Evans' arms, then at Gary, then at Fliss. 'What's all this about, Felicity Morgan – what's happened to Ellie-May?'

'Sir, she came up again. To go in the cupboard, only it's not a cupboard. Look.' She pointed, and then her heart sank. There was no number on the door. 'There was a number, Sir. We all saw it. Thirteen. And Ellie-May opened it and it opened inwards, and inside –' She stopped. There was disbelief in the teacher's eyes, and the hard glint of anger. She dashed across to the door, twisted the knob and pushed.

It was locked. She pulled, but the door didn't move. She turned, pointing. 'Look at Ellie-May's neck, Sir!'

'Yes, look at it,' said Mrs Evans, grimly. She tilted the girl's head to one side and lifted the hair. Ellie-May's neck was bruised and scratched.

'She was fighting, Miss – fighting to get in the room. We had to stop her, Miss.'

'That's enough!' Mrs Evans glared at Fliss. 'If Ellie-May came up here of her own accord, then she was obviously walking in her sleep. It's quite common among young people, and all you had to do was come down and tell me or one of the other teachers. Instead, it seems to me that you woke her in a sudden, violent way and she panicked, as anybody would. You've been silly and irresponsible, and there's to be no more of it. Go to your beds, and in the morning I'll want to know what you, Gary Bazzard, and you, David Trotter, were

**118**

doing up here on the girls' landing in the middle of the night.'

Ellie-May was helped to her feet and taken away, supported by Mrs Marriott on one side and Mrs Evans on the other. Gary and Trot followed a grim-faced Mr Hepworth downstairs, and Fliss and Lisa were left gazing at each other, nonplussed.

'What can we do?' whispered Lisa, almost crying. 'Nobody believes us.'

Fliss sighed and shook her head. 'I don't know, Lisa. I'm too tired and fed up and scared to think. We'll talk in the morning.'

She crept into bed, and jumped when Marie's voice came out of the darkness. 'What happened?'

Fliss sighed. 'Nothing, Marie. Nothing much, anyway. I'll tell you tomorrow, OK?'

'Promise?'

'Promise.'

'OK.'

She expected to lie awake till dawn, but she didn't. She had just time to wonder in a muzzy way what she was going to tell Marie, before sleep rolled in like a black tide and bore her away.

Thursday dawned clear and sunny after the rain. Ellie-May appeared at breakfast, smiling wanly and saying she was feeling much better. Fliss watched her across the dining-room and wondered if she remembered anything at all about last night. From the way she was behaving, it seemed she did not.

Practically everybody had heard something of the disturbance – even the boys on the first floor – and the talk over breakfast was mostly about sleepwalking. Fliss had told Marie that Ellie-May had been found on the top landing, sleepwalking, and had reacted badly to being woken up. Trot and Gary, she said, were in trouble because they had done the waking. When Marie asked what the boys were doing on the top landing in the first place, she said they'd seen Ellie-May pass their floor and followed her up. It didn't sound too convincing to Fliss, but it had got around.

Trot and Gary had been interviewed by Mrs Evans before breakfast. When Trot started to tell her what he saw as he reached for the door to pull it closed, she cut him off, saying, 'The door opens outwards, David, and anyway it was locked.' And when Gary said there was a vampire in the hotel, she told him not to be so stupid. 'If I catch you spreading that story among the other children,' she said, 'a letter will go to your parents the minute we get back to school.'

They were lucky in a way though. Mrs Evans decided they'd gone to the top floor because they were worried about Ellie-May. 'There was absolutely no need for you to worry,' she told them, 'but I can see you were trying to be helpful, so we'll say no more about it.'

So, in spite of the midnight rumpus, and against all the odds, the four found themselves back in favour, free to join in the day's activities. It was to be a busy day, and Fliss hoped this might help her to forget the horrors of the night. This morning they were taking the coach six miles to Robin Hood's Bay where, according to Mr Hepworth, there was a good beach and quaint, narrow streets. At twelve o'clock they would return to Whitby for a fish-and-chip lunch on the seafront, before being turned loose to do their shopping in the afternoon.

Robin Hood's Bay was good. The sun shone all morning and they ran along the sand and played hide-and-seek up and down the little streets. By the time they piled back on to the coach, everybody had worked up an appetite and fish and chips sounded just right.

When they arrived back in Whitby, the teachers got the children settled on some benches not far from the jetty, and Mr Hepworth chose a boy and a girl to go with him to the chippy. Fliss knew he wouldn't pick her – not after last night – and he didn't. He chose John Phelan and Vicky Holmes, and the three of them went across the road and tagged on the back of the queue. Fliss watched. The service was fast, but the queue didn't get any shorter because people kept joining it. She smiled to herself, wondering what the people behind would say when old Hepworth ordered fish and chips thirty-four times with salt and vinegar.

It took them ten minutes to get served and come staggering back with armfuls of greasy little packets. Mrs Evans and Mrs Marriott gave out the portions, and everybody sat in the sunshine munching, chatting and throwing scraps to a gang of gulls which appeared out of nowhere, on the scrounge.

Gary looked at Fliss. 'Where are you going first when they turn us loose, Fliss?'

She shrugged. 'I don't know. A gift shop, I suppose – I want to get a pressy for my mum.'

'I'm not,' he told her. 'I'm off round that "Dracula Experience" place we saw the other day.'

Fliss pulled a face. 'Haven't you had enough of that sort of thing in real life? I know I have.'

'No! I know what you mean, but this is different – a bit of fun. And anyway, I might find a clue there to the mystery of room thirteen.'

'Will you heck! Anyway, I'm not going – it's the last place I want to be.'

'You're chicken, that's why.'

'Am I hummer! Chicken of some daft show after what we've seen at The Crow's Nest? You must be joking.'

'Come on then – prove it.'

'No way.'

'Like I said – chicken.'

'Naff off, Gary, you div!'

'Chicken!'

'OK then – I'll come, and I bet you're more chicken than me. You were scared spitless Tuesday night – I could tell.'

He scoffed. 'You were, you mean.'

The argument might have continued for ever if Mrs Evans hadn't called everybody together to speak to them. Fish-and-chip wrappers had been gathered up and deposited in bins, and the place left tidy as always.

'Right. This is it – the moment you've all been waiting for. You are free to go off now with your friends and spend what's left of your pocket-money. You may go into shops or, if you must, into amusement arcades, but you must stay on the seafront, on this side of the bridge. There's to be no crossing into the old town, and nobody is to go wandering off up the streets leading to the West Cliff. Mrs Marriott, Mr Hepworth and I will be keeping our eyes open, and we don't expect to see anybody charging along the pavements, shouting. Remember, there are other people here besides yourselves, and they don't want to be shoved into the roadway or deafened by children yelling. And please – ' her face changed, so that she looked to be in great pain, 'think before you buy. Seaside shops are full of cheap, tinselly rubbish which looks tempting, but falls apart if you breathe on it. There are nice things – good things – you can take home to your parents, but you have to look for them. Off you go, then.'

Fliss felt like slipping away with Lisa to look in shop windows, but Gary wouldn't let her. 'Come on,' he demanded. 'You said you weren't chicken, so let's go. Last one there's a plonker.'

In spite of Gary's taunting, neither Trot nor Lisa came with them. The only ones who agreed to come were Gemma Carlisle, and Grant Cooper, who arrived last but offered to break the face of the first person who called him a plonker. They paid their fifty pences and went in.

The first bit was a sort of shop, with mugs, T-shirts and badges for sale. 'Huh!' snorted Gary, 'I don't call this scary.' He bought a badge with a bat on it, and they moved on into a dark tunnel. 'This is more like it,' said Gemma. As she spoke, there was a blood-curdling scream and something brushed Fliss's cheek. She ducked away with a cry, and Grant and Gary laughed at her. They were wading through some sort of smoke or vapour which swirled low down, hiding their feet. In the tunnel walls were windows through which weird scenes could be seen. In one, a coffin-lid was lifted by a ghastly hand. In another, a woman with bloodstained clothing lay on a bed, while a red-eyed vampire leered at her through her window. While Fliss gazed at this scene, wishing she was somewhere else, a hand came out of the darkness. Shrinking from it, she walked right into another which grabbed at her throat. She recoiled and started walking faster, wanting only to get to the end of the tunnel and out into the sunlight. But now the floor was moving, and she had to walk fast just to stay where she was. It was like her dream. She wanted to go one way, but her feet were taking her another. Sobbing, she broke into a run, and after a moment the moving section was behind her. She looked down, and the floor was glass. Under the glass was soil, and in the soil, half-embedded, lay the half-rotted heads of corpses.

She hurried on, feeling sick, looking straight in front of her, thinking, I shouldn't have come. I should never have let that idiot Gary persuade me. She was sweating. The screams were getting louder, and there was a sudden gust of wind. She didn't know where the others were, and she didn't care. She rushed along, her hair and face brushed by unseen things. Through her eye-corners she glimpsed spiders and graves and the toothy grins of skeletons.

She blundered on, and then at last she saw a door with a sign on it. WAY OUT.

Thank goodness. Oh, thank goodness! She pushed. It swung open. No sunlight. No. Darkness, and a standing corpse whose head fell off as she watched.

She swerved and rushed past with her head down, and here was another corpse, blocking the way. She swerved again, and it stuck out a pale, bony hand. Sudden anger rose in her against this ridiculous place, and her own stupidity in coming here. Teeth bared, she struck at the hand, but it caught her wrist and the corpse whispered, 'Wait – I have to talk to you.'

She screamed, snatching back her hand. The corpse made a small, distressed sound like the mew of a kitten, and in that instant Fliss recognized it. It wasn't a corpse. It was the old woman in the shelter. Mad Sal Haggerlythe.

'What – what d'you want?'

'Here – back here where there's nobody.' The old woman took her wrist again, gently this time, and led her through a gap in the tunnel wall. It was dark and cold and seemed to be a sort of storage space, with planks and trestles and paint cans, and a lot of stuff she couldn't quite make out. There was a musty smell.

'Where's this?' She didn't know why she'd allowed herself to be led here – if she'd resisted there'd have been nothing the old hag could have done about it.

'Behind the tunnel,' Sal whispered, 'in the real world.' She chuckled wheezily. 'Folks walk through tunnels all their lives, y'know. All their lives. Gawping in through lighted windows, thinking what they see's real, but it's not.' She laughed again. 'No, it's not. They're in a tunnel, see. Looking at a show. And all the time, the real world's just inches away through the wall. And now and then, just now and then, somebody finds a hole and goes through and sees what's behind it all, and d'you know what they get called then?'

The old woman paused, and Fliss shook her head.

'Mad, that's what. Barmy. They're the ones who know what really goes on – what it's all made of – and they call 'em mad. Lock 'em away, some of 'em. I 'spect they'll come for me one of these days. D'you know what i'm talking about?'

Fliss shook her head again, in the dark. 'No. Not really. I'm sorry.' She wondered where Gemma was, and Gary, and Grant. Out by now, probably. She wanted to be with them. 'Look – I've got to go. My friends'll wonder where I am.'

'Listen, then. You've seen something, haven't you, at The Crow's Nest – something strange? And there's a sick child?'

'Yes,' Fliss murmured, 'but how did you know?'

'I know, because I lived in that place a long time ago, before the Great War. It was East View then, not The Crow's Nest. I went there when I was ten, as a scullery maid. It was a grand house then. Turnbull, they called the people who had it. Mr and Mrs Turnbull and their little daughter, Margaret. It wasn't an hotel, you understand – it was a house. A private residence. You've seen the abbey, haven't you?'

Fliss nodded. 'Yesterday.' She wished the woman would come to the point and let her go. If there was a point. There might not be. That was probably one of the signs of madness. It occurred to her that Sal might be dangerous, and she wondered if she'd find her way back to the tunnel if she had to run.

'Well,' the old woman went on, 'there was a bit more to it when I was your age. A gateway, with a little house. Children kept well away from that gateway after dark, I can tell you. Grown-ups too, come to that. That's where he was, see?'

'Who?'

'Him that's in The Crow's Nest now.'

'Who's in The Crow's Nest? Who is he?'

'I think you know. Anyway, that's where he was. Old gatehouse. Folks who knew, steered clear. Strangers didn't. Not always. Now and then, someone'd vanish. Drownded, we'd say. Fell over the cliff in the dark. We knew better. Anyway, it come nineteen-fourteen, and the Great War. Near Christmas, a German battleship comes and stands off a mile or two and fires on the Coastguard Station. Some of the shells hit the abbey. One gets the gateway, and demolishes the little house. Doesn't demolish him, though, 'cause there's only one way to do that, and you know what that is. Anyhow, he's lost his place and so there he is, in the middle of the night, seeking another. He's got to find it before first light, and you know why. And out of all the houses in the town, he picks East View, and that's the end of it.'

'End of it – how d'you mean?'

'End of it as a place folks can live in in peace. Listen. Margaret Turnbull – little Meg – the apple of her daddy's eye. She falls sick. All through that winter, paler and paler, thinner and thinner. Calling out in her sleep. Doctors come. Specialists. No improvement. Comes a night in early spring, and there's ever such a bang and a clatter and they find her at the foot of the stair, unconscious. Seven year old. Doctor says she's been walking in her sleep. Anyway, the little mite recovers, though it's touch and go for a while, and the minute she's strong enough Master Turnbull sells up and moves on, and we're all let go. Later, we hear the child perks up like magic as soon as she's away from that house. And after that the place stands empty, and folks steer clear, same as they used to with the gatehouse. Somebody comes along and buys it eventually – a stranger, but he has no luck and moves out. Place has kept changing hands ever since. Soldiers were billeted there in the last war, and one disappeared.

Deserted, says the authorities. Or drownded, we say, but it's neither. And now he's got bairns – a fresh lot practically every week, and he'll be laughing, and it's you've got to stop his laughter, Miss.'

'Me?' Fliss peered at old Sal in the gloom. 'Why me? And anyway, how?'

'Why you?' The old woman poked a bony finger into her middle. 'Because you had the dream, that's why. You know – the Gate of Fate. The Keep of Sleep. The Room of Doom and the Bed of Dread. Remember?'

Fliss nodded, shivering. 'Yes.' Her voice was a croak. 'But how –?'

'How do I know? I told you. I can go through the wall. Leave the tunnel. See what's really what. And as for how, you'll be told. Don't ask me who'll tell you, because I couldn't explain – just like you can't explain any of this to your teachers – but believe me, you'll be told. And if you refuse to do it – if you don't do what has to be done – your little friend is doomed, together with those who went before her and all who'll follow. Doomed to wander the earth, for ever. Do you understand what I'm saying, Felicity?'

'You know my name.'

'Oh, yes. Felicity. It means happiness. Did you know that?'

'No, I didn't.'

'Well, that's what it means. And if you can be very brave tonight, you'll let happiness back into that sad house, and into the hearts of more people than you know. Will you do it, Felicity?'

Fliss hesitated. The old woman's words were whirling around inside her head. Strange words. A madwoman's words. Yes, Sal Haggerlythe was mad all right – no doubt about it – completely out of her tree. And yet she knew so many things. The dream. All that stuff in The Crow's Nest. Her name, and what it meant.

She nodded, biting her lip. 'Yes.'

'Good.' A frail hand fell on her shoulder and squeezed. 'You'll succeed, Felicity. I know you will. Off you go now – your friends are worrying.'

Fliss allowed old Sal to take her hand and steer her back to the hole in the wall. Two people passed by, laughing to show they weren't scared. Sal waited till they'd gone by, then whispered, 'Follow them – they're on their way out.' Fliss felt a gentle push in the small of her back. She followed the laughing pair, and when she looked round a moment later, there was nothing to be seen.

**24**

'Where the heck have you been? We've been waiting ages.'

Fliss had emerged, blinking against the sudden glare, on a narrow street at the back of the building. Gemma, Grant and Gary, keen to move on to the next thing, gazed reproachfully at her.

'Sorry. I got lost.'

'Lost?' sneered Gemma. 'How could you get lost in a tunnel, for goodness sake. You walk through and that's it.'

'And you were miles in front of us,' put in Grant. 'We expected to find you waiting here when we got out.'

Gary grinned. 'You shot off up that tunnel in a heck of a hurry, Fliss. For someone who's not chicken, I mean.'

'Chicken's got nothing to do with it. It was that moving floor. It was like a dream I had – a nightmare. My feet taking me where I didn't want to go.

And then there was this hole in the wall, and I went through and I was behind the tunnel. It was pitch black, and I kept bumping into stuff – rubbish and that. I thought I'd never find my way out.'

'You're a nut,' said Grant. 'I never saw any hole, and if I had I wouldn't have gone through. Anyway, where we going next – amusements?'

Gary shook his head. 'Not me. I don't like fruit machines. You lose all your money. I'm off to the shops.'

'Me too,' said Fliss. She needed to talk to Gary, away from the other two.

'Well, I'm going with Grant,' said Gemma. 'I won two pounds for ten pence on a machine last year, at Blackpool.'

When Grant and Gemma had gone, Fliss said, 'I've got something to tell you, Gary.'

'What?' They were back on the seafront, heading for the gift shops. Gary was walking fast.

'Slow down a bit and I'll tell you. It's not the flipping Olympics, you know.'

Gary stopped. 'Go on then – what?'

She told him about Sal Haggerlythe, and what the old woman had said. When she'd told him about the promise she'd made, she said, 'Will you help me, Gary? I don't think I'd attempt it by myself.'

Gary pulled a face. 'I guess so. I mean, we've been together all the way along, haven't we? Trot and Lisa too. I just don't know what it is we're supposed to do, Fliss.'

'She said we'd be told.'

'Yeah, but she's barmy, isn't she? If I hadn't seen all that weird stuff with my own eyes, I wouldn't believe a word she said.'

'But you have seen it. Old Sal might be mad, Gary, but she knows all about The Crow's Nest.'

'Hmm. Well, we'll just have to wait and see if we're told, won't we? If we're not, I don't see how we can do anything except keep Ellie-May from going in that cupboard.'

They shopped. Fliss bought a brown photo mounted on a block for her parents. It was by somebody called Sutcliffe, who lived a long time ago and was a famous photographer. It showed two children playing with a toy boat. She'd seen one like it, but bigger, on the wall at The Crow's Nest.

Gary found a leather key-fob with the abbey and the word Whitby embossed on it for his dad, and a little vase encrusted with seashells for his mum.

By the time they'd decided on these purchases, it was half-past two. They were due to meet the teachers back at the bandstand at three, so they made their way in that direction and spent the last twenty minutes in the lifeboat museum. Some of the others were there too, and they compared presents and donated their last few pennies to the lifeboats.

At three, Fliss, Gary and the others left the museum and crossed the road to the bandstand, where the teachers were waiting. Nearly everybody was there. The twins weren't, and neither was Trot. Everybody sat down except Mrs Evans, who stood gazing along the seafront and looking at her watch.

The twins turned up. Mrs Evans frowned at them. 'What time were we to meet?' she asked.

'Three o'clock, Miss,' murmured Joanne.

'And what time is it now, Joanne?'

'Miss, eight minutes past. We were on the donkeys, Miss.'

'Hmmm.'

It was almost a quarter-past three when Trot came trudging up the slipway from the beach. He was carrying a torn plastic kite, and looked fed up.

'And where have you been, David Trotter? Do you know what the time is?'

'Yes, Miss. Sorry, Miss. I was trying to mend my kite.'

Mrs Evans looked at the kite. It was made of clear polythene on a rigid plastic frame. It had a picture of a bat on it, but the polythene was badly torn and hung in tatters from its frame. She sighed. 'What was the last thing I said before we went off to do our shopping, David?'

'I don't know, Miss.'

'No, because you weren't listening. I warned everybody not to spend money on cheap, rubbishy goods, David. How much was that kite?'

'One pound forty, Miss.'

'One pound forty, and look at it. Didn't you notice how thin that polythene was? Didn't you realize that the first good gust of wind would rip it to pieces?'

'No, Miss.'

'No, Miss. Well, it did, didn't it?' She turned to the group. 'You know, I sometimes wonder whether the other teachers and myself aren't just wasting our breath talking to you people. First there was Lisa Watmough, going into a shop before we even got here, buying a trashy flashlight which is probably broken already. Then Gary Bazzard spends I don't know how much on a stick of rock the size of a telegraph pole.' Her eyes found Gary, who looked surprised. 'Oh, yes, Gary – I know all about that rock. It's in your room now, melting, with a beard of bed-fluff on it. You've sucked at it till you're sick of it, and now you don't know what to do with it.' She looked at

Trot again. 'And now you, with your kite. I only hope that next time, if there is a next time, you'll be told.'

You'll be told. Fliss, whose mind had been wandering, looked up sharply. Mrs Evans, talking about –

Buying things. Things you shouldn't. Lisa. Gary. Trot. Why those three? It's a connection, isn't it? Must be. Can't be coincidence, can it? Her heart kicked. You'll be told.

Yeah, but hold on a minute. What about me? I'm one of them. I started it, in fact, and I haven't been in trouble for buying anything. I've been late for breakfast, but that's different. Nobody's said to me, 'You shouldn't have bought that, it's rubbish.' Nobody's –

The pebble. The big pebble. I didn't buy it, of course, but Mrs Evans told me to put it down, and it's a thing, like a torch or a stick of rock or a kite.

That's it. The four of us. Nobody else has been told off for something they've got, have they? She sat, frowning, gnawing her lip.

A torch. A stick of rock. A pebble. A kite.

You'll be told.

138

25

They were back at The Crow's Nest by twenty to four, stowing their purchases in their rooms and writing up their journals. It had been their last day, and Fliss wondered why it had had to end so early. It wasn't as if they'd be setting off home at the crack of dawn and needed an early night. They weren't leaving till half-past ten.

Not that an early night would be much use to the four of us anyway, she thought. She had talked briefly to Lisa and Trot on the stairway. They knew what had happened to her today, and had agreed to meet Gary and herself in the usual spot at half-past eleven.

The rest of the kids were feeling a bit down because the holiday was nearly over, but for Fliss, Gary, Lisa and Trot it couldn't end soon enough. They were tired and frightened, and wanted only to be near their parents and to sleep in their own beds.

'Guess what?' said Marie. She was looking out of the window.

'Shut up, Marie,' growled Maureen. 'I'm trying to write.'

'The old witch is there again,' said Marie, ignoring her.

'We know,' said Joanne, impatiently. 'We saw her when we came past the shelter just now. How d'you spell "stake", Fliss?'

Fliss looked up. 'There's two sorts of stake,' she said. 'What're you writing about?'

'A poster I saw in the town. Movie poster. It showed this vampire with a stake through its heart. It said, "Party all night, sleep all day, never grow old, never die, it's fun being a vampire."'

'That sort of stake's S-T-A-K-E,' Fliss told her.

'Thanks.' Joanne bent her head over her work. Marie left the window, sat down at the dressing-table and began to write. Silence reigned.

Fliss chewed her pencil and stared at the carpet. S-T-A-K-E. Stake. A short pole, sharpened at one end, and a mallet to hammer it in with. A flaming torch to illuminate the crypt, and a cross lest the vampire should wake. A stick of rock the size of a telegraph pole, sucked to a point. A pebble too heavy for the pocket. A torch the shape of a dragon. A cross? No cross.

Trot. We've each done our bit, except Trot. Trot must find the cross, then. He hasn't got one that I've ever seen. He didn't buy one today, which was the last chance. He bought –

A kite. That tattered kite on its rigid, cross-shaped frame. That's it!

She was certain, now. You'll be told, Sal Haggerlythe had said, and it was true. Mrs Evans had catalogued the items, and then spoken those very words. You'll be told. The pieces fitted. Every one.

She got up and went to the window. Sal was sitting in the shelter, and seemed to be looking at her. Fliss mouthed a silent 'yes,' and nodded. The woman made no response, but then, the sun was behind the hotel and this side was in shadow.

When they went down to the lounge, the children found out why they'd returned early to the hotel. There was to be a disco for them in the dining-room starting at seven o'clock. They would eat early so that the room could be prepared, and would have plenty of time to wash, do their hair and get into their best outfits before the festivities began.

'It's a farewell disco,' Mr Hepworth told them. 'Farewell to The Crow's Nest, farewell to Whitby. We've kept it a secret till now because we wanted it to be a surprise. It will go on until half-past nine, with a break at eight o'clock for pop, crisps and various other goodies. Mr and Mrs Wilkinson's daughter will be running the disco, and I think it's very kind of them all. Don't you?'

Everybody did. There were three very loud cheers for the Wilkinsons, who came to the doorway of the lounge to hear them, and then it was dinnertime.

As she ate, Fliss watched Ellie-May, two tables away. She'd joined them on the trip to Robin Hood's Bay that morning, and had seemed fine. She'd behaved so normally that at one point Fliss had approached her and spoken, just to see what she'd do. Ellie-May had been her usual rude self, telling Fliss to drop dead, and she seemed normal now too, sitting between Tara and Michelle, boasting about the outfit she was going to wear. She's chuffed to little mint balls, thought Fliss. Looking forward to the disco like everybody else. She doesn't remember a thing about last night. Or the night before. Or the night before that.

Lucky her.

**26**

'Hey, where's the dining-room gone?' Neil Atkinson, first down in jeans and sneakers, paused in the doorway. Tables and carpet had disappeared. Chairs had been moved back against the walls. Heavy curtains blacked out all the windows. Coloured lights flashed red, then blue, then green, striking sparks from the parquet, leaving corners in shadow. The place looked twice as big as before. At one end, between stacked speakers, a girl stood behind a double-deck. She twitched and writhed as Madonna belted out a number so loud you felt it through your feet.

'Wow!' Sarah-Jane, made-up and dressed to kill, went on tiptoe to peer over the boy's shoulder. 'It's brilliant – like a real disco. What we waiting for?'

They walked out on to the floor, fitting their movements into the beat, beginning to dance. The girl at the deck smiled as her blue face turned to

143

green. Others followed, spilling on to the floor in their finery with grins and exclamations.

It grew hot as record followed record, rising and falling on the twin-deck in unbroken series. The three teachers sat together way back in shadow and watched. Now and then, somebody would go over and try to get them to dance, but they wouldn't. 'My dancing days are over,' they'd say, or, 'I'm waiting for Buddy Holly.' When the break came at eight, everybody was ready for it.

Fliss managed to get the other three in a corner together. Gary had worked up a sweat. His hair was stuck to his forehead. He slurped Coke as she told them what she'd worked out. When she'd finished, he said, 'So what you're saying is, we go in there where he is, and all we've got is a torch, a pebble, a stick of rock and a knackered kite, right?'

Fliss nodded.

'Well, I don't fancy it, I can tell you that.'

'Who does, but have you got a better idea?'

'Sure. We go to bed tonight like everybody else and forget it.'

'And what about Ellie-May? Not to mention all the other kids he's enticed into that cupboard, and all those he will in future if we don't do something about it.'

'It's got nothing to do with us, has it? We've done our best. We tried to tell the teachers but they wouldn't listen. What I mean is, here we are at this disco, right? And everybody's really enjoying it except us. It's been the same all week. Everybody else has been on holiday, but we've been in the middle of a nightmare. Why us, Fliss? Tell me that.'

Fliss shrugged. 'I can't. I don't know why us, Gary, except we've been picked out somehow. You bought that rock and spent three days sucking it to a point. You're part of the team.'

'Big deal.'

She looked him in the eye. 'We can't do it without you, Gary. It needs four. Four things, four people. Are you chickening out?'

He shook his head, looking at the floor. 'I don't suppose so. It's not fair, that's all I'm saying.'

'You'll be there though, at half-eleven?'

'Yes.'

The second half kicked off with the new Bros album. They danced together, the four of them, a little apart from the others. Gary was right, of course. Deep down, each of them felt as he did – that they'd been unfairly singled out. They'd do what had to be done, but their week had been ruined and that was that. They moved mechanically to the music and thought about midnight.

The end came too soon for everybody, except perhaps the teachers, who had sat it all out, waiting in vain for Buddy Holly. At half-past nine the last track faded, the lights came on and the enchantment melted away. Children stood on the scuffed, littered floor, exposed, self-conscious and tired. Mr Hepworth led three cheers and a round of applause for the disc jockey, who grinned, blushed and looked at her feet. After that, they collected jackets, bags and cardigans and went away to bed.

Mrs Evans stuck her head round the door just as Fliss was taking her shoes off. 'Can I see you out here a minute, please, Felicity?'

Fliss sighed, re-tying the laces. 'What's up now, I wonder?'

'You're in bother,' said Marie, cheerfully. She was already in bed. The twins hadn't finished in the bathroom yet.

Fliss went out on to the landing. Mrs Evans had Lisa there too. She spoke quietly to them both.

'Now listen. I know you're both worried about Ellie-May Sunderland, but you needn't worry any more. She's been fine today, but anyway Mrs Marriott and I have decided to take her into our room for the night, just in case she decides to go sleepwalking again. Mr Hepworth is speaking to Gary and David, and we want you all in bed and asleep before the clock strikes ten. Is that clear?'

'Yes, Miss.'

The disco had shattered everybody, and by the time the faraway clock struck ten Marie and the twins were fast asleep. Fliss lay stroking her pebble, wishing she could sleep too. She could have, easily, but she knew if she did she wouldn't wake up till morning.

So. Ellie-May won't be coming. That doesn't mean the room out there won't change though – wish it did. What about the others? Mr Hepworth's spoken to Trot and Gary. They know Ellie-May's being guarded. Will it stop them coming? Gary wasn't too keen to begin with. And if they don't come, what do we do, Lisa and me? Shine the torch in his eyes and hit him with the pebble, or call it off and let him go on luring kids to their doom? And anyway, who says Lisa's going to show up?

Good way to keep awake, worrying like this. Every quarter that clock chimes, but it seems like hours between. Ten fifteen. Ten thirty. Ten forty flipping five. Forty-five minutes to go.

Then what?

They came. All of them. Fliss came last, clutching her pebble.

'Have we all got our stuff?' she whispered. They showed her. 'Right.' She looked at her watch. Twenty to twelve. 'Soon be over now.'

'Aye,' growled Gary. 'One way or the other.'

Fliss looked at him. 'We're going to succeed, right?'

He shrugged. 'If you say so. But if somebody had told me last week I'd be risking my life for Ellie-May Sunderland I'd have told him he was nuts. I don't even like her, for Pete's sake.'

'Who does, but it's not just for Ellie-May, Gary. Old Sal says it's for all the others.'

'Yeah, well, like I said before, she's crackers.'

They waited. Fliss kept looking at her watch. When it said five to twelve she whispered, 'Right. Time to get into position.'

They'd worked it all out beforehand. Trot was first. He opened the bathroom door and stood on the threshold, holding his kite. He'd stripped away the tattered polythene. All that remained was a stiff, white plastic cross. As soon as the number appeared on the cupboard door, he was to cross the landing, open the door quietly and walk in, holding up the cross. That was in case the vampire was awake and out of his coffin. If he was, then they wouldn't be able to carry out their plan, but the cross might keep the creature at bay till they could get out and slam the door.

Behind Trot stood Lisa with the torch. She would follow him in, and shine the torch around to see if the vampire was loose. If he was, she'd try to dazzle him while they retreated. If he was in the coffin, she was to shine it on his chest, right where Gary had to place the stick of rock.

Gary was third. He would follow the other two in, and if everything was all right, he'd grip his rock with both hands and place the point directly over the vampire's heart.

Fliss would be last. If the vampire was out of the coffin, her job would be to get out fast and that was all. If he was in the coffin, she would raise the pebble and bring it down on the rock, driving the point into the vampire. She was to hammer the rock again and again till the vampire was dead.

It would all have to be done very quickly. Fliss wished they'd been able to practise a couple of times, but they hadn't. So. They had to get it right first time, or else –

The town clock began to chime. 'Stand by,' whispered Fliss from the rear. Her mouth was bone-dry. Her left hand was resting on Gary's shoulder and she could feel him trembling. In front of him, Lisa switched on her torch and trained it on the door.

The pale stain appeared. Four pairs of eyes watched it form the number thirteen. As the figures grew clear, Fliss hissed, 'Go!'

Swiftly, silently, they padded in line across the landing. Trot twisted the doorknob, pushed, and walked into the darkness, holding the cross up high and with Lisa at his heels. The torch beam made a quick sweep of the room and steadied on the long, pale box. Gary strode forward and leaned over the open coffin, grasping the rock in both hands. Fliss stood poised, the great pebble raised high above her head. The torch beam slid over the rim of the box.

He lay with his hands crossed on this breast and his eyes closed. He was thin, and small, and dirty. His face was dead white, except for a dark smudge on the forehead and a brown crust about the bluish lips. A fleece of pale, tangled hair, grey with dust, covered the skull, falling on to the bed of earth which covered the bottom of the coffin. His fingernails were split and blackened, and a disgusting smell rose from the single, filthy garment he wore, which looked like a nightshirt or shroud.

'Ugh!' Gary's stomach heaved and he twisted his face aside.

'Quick!' hissed Lisa. 'His eyes are moving – look!'

As she spoke, the vampire's eyelids fluttered. Gary sucked in some air, turned back and planted the spike he'd made in the vee between the creature's hands. The vampire's eyes flew open, red-rimmed, filled with fear. Grabbing the coffin-rim with one hand and scrabbling in the earth with the other, he began to rise. His lips parted. Chipped, yellow fangs glistened in the torchlight and the breath hissed stinking through his teeth. Trot dashed forward and thrust his cross at the contorted face. The vampire let go of the coffin-rim to strike at it, and as he did so Gary threw all this weight forward, bore down on the spike and yelled, 'Now, Fliss – now!'

Fliss aimed, screwed up her eyes and brought the pebble down with all the force she could muster. There was a wet thud and the vampire began to scream, bucking and thrashing so violently that the coffin slid about. Gary fell forward across the table, clinging desperately to the spike. 'Again!' he gasped. 'For Pete's sake hit it again, Fliss!'

Fliss, sickened, raised the pebble and brought it down again, driving the spike clear through the writhing body into the bloody earth beneath, where it broke off. The vampire screamed again, clutching at the coffin-rim with both hands, flailing its naked legs and arching its back so violently that Gary's grip was broken and he crashed to the floor.

At once the others closed in. Lisa's beam lanced into the creature's fear-crazed eyes. Trot lowered the cross till it almost touched the coffin-rim, and Fliss lifted the pebble, ready to split the vampire's skull.

She didn't have to. As they watched the creature's struggles began to subside. Its screams became ghastly, bubbling cries as it twisted this way and that, clutching at the impaling spike, striving to draw it out. Soon, weakening, it ceased to kick.

Its hands lost their grip on the spike and slid down the curve of the heaving chest on the glistening earth. It lay, mouth open, gulping at the air, rolling its head and screwing up its eyes as it strove to avoid the light. Gradually its movements became sluggish and its breathing shallow. Then, quite suddenly it seemed, the breathing stopped.

The head rolled over to one side. All movement ceased.

Fliss lowered her arms, dropped the pebble on the table and turned away. Trot let his cross fall to the floor and stood, gazing into the coffin. Gary had picked himself up and was leaning against the wall with this eyes closed, breathing hard, whispering, 'We did it. Wow, we did it,' over and over. Lisa aimed her torch beam at the floor and very slowly followed the puddle of light towards the open door. As she did so there were footfalls on the stair, and voices, and the landing light triggered the shift, so that three frowsy teachers saw four dishevelled children and a cupboard which was locked.

Some mornings are just perfect. You know what I mean. You've slept like a log, you come wide awake and it's sunshine from the word go. Sunshine and birdsong and your favourite breakfast and everybody being nice to you. It sometimes happens to people on their birthday.

Well, that Friday morning at Whitby was one of those, and it wasn't anybody's birthday. There should have been some gloom about because the holiday was over, but there wasn't. Fliss and the other three should have felt dog-tired and maybe a little bit chastened after their horrific adventure, but they didn't. They'd got a terrific telling-off from old Hepworth, of course, but they didn't mind that. An enormous weight had been lifted from them and they walked on air. Nobody thought, Oh, crikey, school. Everybody thought, Oh great, home! It was that sort of morning.

Fliss was hungry. The aroma of sausages, drifting up from the basement kitchen, made her mouth water. Sausages! Her favourite. The cereal was a favourite, too. She shovelled it into her face, watching the teachers.

They hadn't tried to explain to the teachers. There was no point. Grown-ups don't believe anything you tell them. They have to see with their own eyes, and there was nothing to see. Not now.

After breakfast, the children went upstairs to finish packing and tidy their rooms. The door of the linen cupboard was closed, and there was no number on it. Never will be again, thought Fliss. Not even at midnight. She smiled.

In room ten, everything had been packed away. Marie and the twins stood looking out of the window. 'There's no old witch today,' said Maureen.

'Mad Sal's not a witch,' said Fliss. 'And she's not mad either.'

Room ten looked bare without their bits and pieces. It wasn't their room any more and they weren't sorry to leave it. They carried their luggage downstairs and stacked it in the hallway. The coach wasn't due for another hour, so the teachers took them down to the beach where they ran or skimmed pebbles or stood, saying goodbye to the sea, which sparkled in the sun.

The coach was coming at half-past ten. At

twenty past, Mr Hepworth called them together and led them back up the steep pathway.

It was there. The driver was stowing the last of the luggage in the boot. Mr Wilkinson was helping him. Both men whistled as they worked.

The children crossed the road and climbed on board. Fliss and Lisa got seats together. The driver slipped into his seat, grinned at the children through his mirror and told them to hold tight. The engine roared into life. The coach rolled forward. The Wilkinsons stood on the top step, waving. The children waved back. The coach gathered speed. The Crow's Nest fell away behind. They were going home.

Fliss settled back in the comfy seat and sighed. 'It's been a funny sort of holiday,' she said.

Lisa nodded. 'You can say that again. I'm glad we did it, though. We made things better, didn't we, Fliss – I could sort of feel it this morning.'

'Oh, so could I. Everybody could, I think. Mr Wilkinson, whistling. And the driver. Drivers are usually a bit narky when they've got a coachload of kids, but this one isn't. Look at him, grinning in the mirror.'

The coach swooped down into Sleights, then toiled up the road to the moors. Halfway up, Fliss slapped her knee and cried, 'Drat!'

Lisa looked at her. 'What's up?'

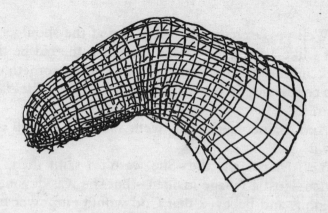

# CHAPTER ONE

Fliss stuck her hand up. 'Why's it called a worm if it was a dragon, Sir?'

Mr Hepworth nodded. 'Good point, Felicity. To us today, the word "worm" conjures up a picture of a small, pink, harmless creature, doesn't it? But in Anglo-Saxon times, dragons and other reptilian monsters were often called worms, so the word would have had pretty dreadful connotations for them. The worm which terrorized Elsworth is said to have been a chain in length and five feet high at the shoulder.'

'How long's a chain, Sir?' asked Grant Cooper.

'Sixty-six feet. That's roughly twenty-two metres.'

'Phew – some worm!'

'Well yes, exactly. And five feet at the shoulder – that's like a fairly big horse, and then there'd be the neck and head, so we're not talking about something you could chop in bits with a garden spade.' The class tittered.

'And Saint Ceridwen went out by herself to face it, Sir?'

'Yes, Marie, she did. She wasn't a saint then, of course – just a village maiden – but she was devoutly religious and believed that God would empower her to overcome the worm, which she called an agent of Satan.'

'I wouldn't have gone, Sir.'

'No, Marie, and neither would I. We don't have Ceridwen's faith, you see.'

'Is it a true story, Sir? I mean, I thought there were no such things as dragons.'

The teacher smiled. 'There are no dragons now, Marie, but this was a thousand years ago, so who knows? Ceridwen certainly existed, and she must have done something pretty remarkable because we know she'd become the most important person in the district by the time she was martyred by the Danes in nine ninety-three.'

David Trotter raised his hand. 'How did she kill the worm, Sir?'

'She didn't. According to the legend, the moment the beast touched the hem of Ceridwen's skirt it became docile, whereupon she commanded it to begone. It slunk away on to the fen and was never seen again.'

Gary Bazzard grinned. 'It might still be out there, Sir.'

'I doubt it, Gary. Elsworth's got you now – it doesn't need another monster.'

'Sir,' said Fliss. 'Why did the Danes kill Ceridwen?'

The teacher shrugged. 'The Danes were pagans, Felicity. When they overran this area they demanded that Ceridwen worship their gods and order her people to do the same. She refused, so they hacked off her limbs and beheaded her.'

'Ugh! And this was exactly a thousand years ago, and that's why the town's having this Festival?'

Mr Hepworth nodded. 'That's correct, and the vicar of St Ceridwen's has invited our school to be involved in various ways, and Mrs Evans and I decided we'd ask Year Eight to perform a re-enactment of Ceridwen's encounter with the worm, and of her martyrdom. It's a great honour – the eyes of the whole town will be on us, so obviously we want to make a first-class job of it and it's all got to be ready in three weeks.'

'So it'll be sort of like doing a play, Sir?'

'That's right, Maureen, and the idea is that you people take a lot of the responsibility yourselves for producing it. Mrs Evans and I will be around if you need us, of course, but we expect you to write a script, do the casting, see to props and costumes and so forth. I think you'll enjoy the experience, but I want you to remember at all times that your finished effort will be seen by practically everybody in Elsworth, so the reputation of Bottomtop Middle is in your hands. That's all, I think. You can go now, and start work as soon as you like.'

'I'm playing the Boss Viking!' cried Gary Bazzard, as Year Eight spilled on to the playground. 'And I'll hack the limbs off anyone who argues.'

Fliss pulled a face at Lisa. 'Old Hepworth must be mad, putting the school's reputation in the hands of guys like him.'

Lisa laughed. 'Gary's a loudmouth, but he's OK. We can always gang up on him - tell him we've got him down to play Ceridwen in a blonde wig and a long white dress.'

That night, Fliss had a dream. In her dream the worm came slithering out of the fenland mist with a thousand-year hunger in its belly and vengeance in its brain and she, cast as Ceridwen by the votes of all her friends, was sent to stand defenceless in its path.

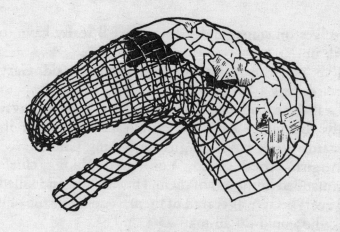

# CHAPTER TWO

They'd learned about the play on Monday. Lunchtime Tuesday there was a class meeting to get the thing off the ground. No teachers were present, though Mrs Evans kept buzzing in and out because they were using her room.

'Right. Now – first things first.' Sarah-Jane Potts, who'd done some acting with a local amateur group, seemed to be chairing the meeting. 'Where will this play be performed?'

'On the Festival Field,' said Tara Matejak. 'Mr Hepworth said so.'

'So the audience will be all round us and there'll be some noise as well. That affects how we arrange ourselves on stage, and it means we'll really have to speak up.'

'I've got this very powerful voice,' said Gary Bazzard. 'It's a Viking Chief's voice, really.'

Sarah-Jane had been tipped off by Lisa and was ready for him. 'Ah well, you can just forget it, Bazzard. We're having a girl for Viking Chief.'

'A girl?' cried Gary. 'You can't. Viking chiefs commanded hundreds of men. They fought and killed and everybody was scared of them. You name me one girl who could do all that.'

'How about Boudicca?'

'Who?'

'Boudicca, queen of the Iceni. She led an army against the Romans. And then there's Cartimandua, queen of the Brigante. She fought the Romans too.'

'You're making it up. You'll be telling me next that Arnold Schwarzenegger never goes anywhere without his knitting.'

'I'm not, and I won't,' retorted Sarah-Jane. 'But the Viking Chief's a girl, and that's that.'

'Which girl?' Gary wasn't about to give up.

'We don't know. We haven't voted yet.'

When they did vote, Gemma got the part. As the result was being announced, Mrs Evans walked in. 'Don't forget your understudies, Sarah-Jane,' she said.

'No way, Miss,' said Sarah-Jane, though she had forgotten.

'What're understudies?' asked Barry Tune.

Mrs Evans smiled. 'An understudy is someone who learns the part of a leading actor or actress, so that he or she can step in and play the part if the star falls ill. It's important to have understudies for all your leading roles – any teacher will tell you that.' She found the book she'd come for and left the room. The class then voted, and Maureen O'Connor was chosen as understudy.

And so it went on. There was consolation for Gary when the class made him worm's head. 'You get to roar, bare your fangs and breathe fire,' Lisa told him. 'What more could anyone ask?'

'If Gary's part of the worm, I want to be in it too,' said David Trotter. He and Gary were best friends. There would be four people in the worm, but there was no voting except for the head. Trot's offer was accepted, and Ellie-May Sunderland and Lisa got the two remaining places. Fliss landed the best part of all, beating Samantha by one vote to play Ceridwen, with Samantha as understudy.

After the allocation of supporting roles, Year Eight turned its attention to the problem of costume. It was decided that people would be responsible for designing and making their own costumes, though some children who were good at sewing would stand by to help if needed. The worm must be twenty-two metres long, and light enough for four people to operate. 'Trouble is, it'll have eight legs,' said Gary. 'Real dragons have four.'

'How the heck do you know?' demanded Fliss. 'Have you seen one?'

'I've seen pictures.'

Fliss snorted. 'I've seen pictures of women with six arms,' she said. 'Doesn't mean women're like that, does it?'

By the time the meeting ended, everybody had something to do. They even had a title for their play: *Ceridwen – Heroine-Saint of Elsworth*. Robert Field had thought it up and everybody liked it. As she walked with Lisa to their own room for register, Fliss felt they'd made a really good start. She hadn't forgotten her nightmare, but in the warm light of afternoon a dream is just a dream.

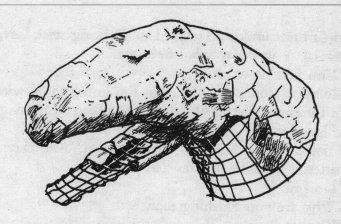

# CHAPTER THREE

'How long did old Hepworth say we'd got?' asked
Lisa, as she and Fliss walked home that afternoon.

'Three weeks, wasn't it?' Fliss began calculating
aloud. 'We're in the first week of April, right? Festival week starts on Saturday the twenty-fourth and
our play's the following Saturday, which is May the
first. So we've got about three weeks by my reckon-
ing. Why?'

'Oh, I was just wondering. There's a lot to do,
isn't there?'

Fliss shrugged. 'Costume to make, lines to learn.
It won't take all that much doing. You don't even
need a costume – they'll only see your legs.'

'I know, but I've got to help with the worm,

15

and I'm not looking forward to working with Gary Bazzard. You know what he's like.'

'You said he was OK.'

'In small doses he's OK, but I'm going to be with him for ages, making the worm and then rehearsing, and I won't even have you to talk to.'

'You'll have Ellie-May.' Fliss grinned. 'And David Trotter. I thought you fancied Trot?'

'Do I heck!'

'Why are you blushing then?'

'I'm not.'

'Oh, I thought you were. Anyway, I'll tell you what.'

'What?'

'If you like, and if the others'll let me, I'll help with the worm.' She smiled. 'My costume's already made, you see.'

Lisa looked at her. 'How d'you manage that?'

'Well, all I need is a long white dress, and I've got one from when I was bridesmaid to my cousin last year. I've been dying for an excuse to wear it.'

'And you'll really come and work on the worm with me?'

'If it's all right with the others, yes.'

'That'll be great, Fliss. We're doing it at Trot's place, in his dad's garage. Apparently there's loads of junk there we can use – wire and old curtains and stuff. Trot says the worm's going to look like

16

one of those dancing lions they have in Thailand – you'll have seen 'em on telly.'

'Yes, I have. I think it's a good idea, but ours'll need a fiercer head. Thai lions don't look scary at all – they're cute and cuddly.' She grinned. 'Like Trot.'

'Shut up.' Lisa kicked a stone into the verge as her cheeks flamed. 'I can't stand him, if you must know.'

'Why did you volunteer for the worm, then?'

'Shut up, Fliss, OK?'

Her friend chuckled. 'OK. When's the first session, Lisa?'

'Tonight. Half-six. You coming?'

'Dunno, do I? Depends how Trot feels really – it's his place. Phone him, then phone me. If he agrees, I'll be there.'

Their ways parted soon after that and Fliss hurried home. It'll be great, she told herself, working with Lisa and the others: creating the monster I'll face on the Festival Field.

So why did I shiver just now?

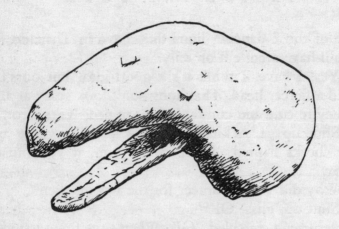

# CHAPTER FOUR

Lisa waited till her watch showed one minute past six, then picked up the phone. Her mum was always telling her it was cheaper after six. She punched in Trot's number, feeling once more the slight tingle of excitement she always got when she did this. It's not true what Fliss says, she told herself. About me and Trot. I like him, that's all. We're friends.

There was a click and Trot's voice said, 'Elsworth four-six-four-two-six-two.'

'Trot? It's Lisa. Listen. Is it all right if Fliss comes tonight? She offered to help with the worm and I said I'd ask you.'

' 'Course it is. Many hands make light work, as my dad would say. Half-six, right?'

'Half-six. See you.' She broke contact and punched in Fliss's number. 'Fliss? Oh, sorry Mrs Morgan, it's Lisa. May I speak to Fliss, please? Thanks. Fliss? Lisa. I called Trot. It's OK for tonight.'

'Great. See you in twenty-five minutes then.'

'Right. 'Bye.'

'I did a rough design,' said Trot, unfolding a sheet of paper.

The four gathered round to see. Mr Trotter had backed his car on to the driveway so they'd have plenty of space.

Ellie-May frowned. 'It looks like a ladder.'

Trot nodded. 'I know, except the rungs are too far apart. This is the basic framework, see? We'd stand in a line with our heads between the rungs and the shafts resting on our shoulders. These hoops,' he pointed, 'are made of wire. They'd run from one shaft to the other like a series of arches, supporting the fabric covering well above our heads and giving the worm's back a nice rounded shape.'

Lisa nodded. 'You're a genius, Trot. It's brilliant.'

Gary nodded. 'Looks sound to me, man. Where do we get the stuff to make it?'

'It's all here.' Trot nodded to where some lengths of timber stood propped in a corner. 'There're the shafts, and we can make rungs from that too. Dad got it to build a porch and never got round to it.

19

And there's a coil of wire for the hoops.'

'What about nails?' asked Fliss.

'Drawerful in the chest there,' Trot told her. 'Staples too, for the hoops. We can have the framework done tonight if we get a move on.'

They did better than that, working together smoothly so that by eight o'clock they had a sturdy framework four metres long and almost a metre in height. They stood, fists on hips, looking at it. 'Four metres,' grunted Gary. 'The real worm was twenty-two.'

'Oh sure,' agreed Trot, 'but a framework that length would be so unwieldy we wouldn't be able to shift it. No, the rest'll be made up of neck and head, and a tail of fabric stiffened with wire.' He laughed. 'What we'll use for the head I don't know.'

'Papier-mâché,' said Fliss. 'It's light, and you can mould it into any shape you want.'

'Take a lot of paper,' said Ellie-May.

'Well, there's five of us,' said Lisa. 'If we get all the newspapers from home and from relatives, we'll have plenty.'

Trot nodded. 'Papier-mâché it is, then. Shall we meet here tomorrow, same time, to make a start?'

Lisa hung around when the others left. It wasn't fair to leave Trot with all the clearing away, and in any case she felt like walking home alone.

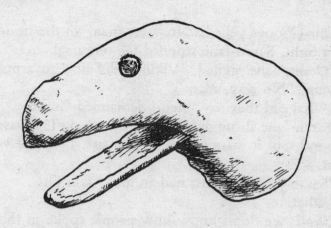

# CHAPTER FIVE

The rest of that week was a busy one for Year Eight. Every spare minute of the school day was spent in discussing the play, and in the evenings the children worked on their costumes. Everybody had a part, as either a villager or a Viking, and the homes of aunts and grandparents were ransacked for materials which might do for a tunic, a helmet or a long dress.

On Thursday afternoon they gave up double games to stage a rough rehearsal on the school field. There were no written parts, so everybody had to make up their lines as they went along. Ad libbing, Sarah-Jane called it, but it wasn't a success. It's not easy thinking up the right words instantly, and when the Viking

Grant Cooper yelled, 'No way, man!' in the middle of a fight, Sarah-Jane stopped the rehearsal.

'Grant,' she sighed, 'Vikings did not go around saying, "No way, man." '

'What did they say, then?' demanded Grant.

Sarah-Jane shrugged. 'I don't know, do I? I wasn't around, but it wasn't "No way, man", I can tell you that.'

'Sarah-Jane, I've just had an idea,' said Fliss.

'What?'

'Well, we don't know how people spoke in those days, do we? Nobody does. So why don't we do it without words?'

Sarah-Jane looked at her. You mean mime it, or do it through dance or something?'

Fliss shook her head. 'No. I thought we could have a narrator. You know – somebody who stands at the side and tells the story as the play unfolds. That way, nobody has to learn lines and we can concentrate on the action.'

'The narrator'd have a lot to memorize.'

'Not necessarily. He or she could read from a script done up to look like an ancient chronicle or something. Nobody'd be watching the narrator anyway, if we made the action exciting enough.'

'Hmmm.' Sarah-Jane frowned. 'It's an idea, Fliss. It'd get rid of "No way, man," and stuff like that, but who's going to do it?'

'I will,' volunteered Andrew Roberts, 'if someone'll help me write it.'

'We'll all help to write it,' smiled Sarah-Jane. 'Thanks, Andrew.'

For the moment they carried on with no words except those of Sarah-Jane, who was directing. They hit another snag after Ceridwen banished the worm. 'What do we do now?' asked Barry Tune. 'I mean, years go by before the Danes come and kill her.'

'Hmmm.' Sarah-Jane frowned again.

'We could have a ceremony,' suggested Waseem. 'You know – the villagers are so grateful to Ceridwen they make her their chief or something.'

'Yes,' put in Haley. 'And remember, the Vikings were raiding long before they settled here. We could show a series of unsuccessful raids with the Danes being repulsed by the villagers.'

Sarah-Jane nodded. 'Good idea, Haley. Yours too, Waseem. Let's try it.'

They tried it, and it worked. Friday lunchtime they went through it again, this time in the hall. The first bit of narration was ready and Andrew read it as they performed. It looked good. 'All we need now is the costumes,' grinned Marie. 'And we're the Royal Shakespeare Company.'

## CHAPTER SIX

Saturday morning Fliss had to go with her mother to buy shoes. Then there was lunch, and by the time she got to Trot's garage the others had practically finished the head. She gasped when she saw it. It was enormous, and looked fantastic with its red eyes and gaping jaws. 'Wow!' she cried. 'Those eyes are really ace, Trot. What're they made of?'

Trot grinned. 'Reflectors, Fliss, from Gary's dad's old car. D'you like 'em?'

'Like 'em? They're amazing. It's like they're staring right at you, hating you. What a terrific idea.'

'Yeah, well – we need a terrific idea from you, Fliss, now that you've finally shown up.'

'Why – what's up?'

'It's the neck,' said Lisa. 'It's designed to go over Gary's head and shoulders and down to his waist, so that the head is firmly supported and won't sway about when the worm's moving.'

'And doesn't it fit?'

'Oh, it fits all right, but it pins Gary's arms to his sides. He feels like an Egyptian mummy in there and it's not safe for him to walk, let alone run. If he tripped, he'd fall flat on his face.'

'Hmmm.' Fliss looked at the head. 'Is the papier-mâché completely dry now?'

'The thickest parts are still a bit soggy, but it's OK. Why?'

'Well, if the neck's dry we could take a saw and cut two slots in it, one either side. It'd still reach his waist back and front, and his arms would be free.'

'Fliss Morgan, you're a genius,' cried Trot. 'An infant prodigy. Why didn't we think of that?'

The slots were quickly cut, and Gary tried on the head. He couldn't see yet because they hadn't made the eye-holes, but they led him on a circuit of the garage and he did some roaring and said he felt much better. Now that the papier-mâché had dried out, the whole thing was surprisingly light. They spent the afternoon painting it, and by half-past four the last scrap of newsprint was covered and the head was a glossy green, except for the inside of the mouth which they'd done with some obscenely pink stuff Ellie-May had got from somewhere. They propped it in a corner and stood in a half-circle, looking at it.

'It looks like a pensioner yawning,' said Lisa. 'It's got no teeth.'

'Don't worry,' said Ellie-May. 'My gran's got some things we can use for teeth.'

'What sort of things?'

'Oh – they're cone-shaped plastic things from where she used to work. Bobbins of some sort, I think. They're all colours, but we can soon paint 'em white.'

Trot looked at her. 'Can you bring them to-morrow?'

'No problem.'

'Right.' He turned to the others. 'Half-past ten then, here?'

This time, Lisa left with Fliss. Fliss grinned. 'Trot found somebody else, has he?'

Lisa shook her head. 'I told you – I don't care about Trot. I care about the play, that's all. I get a funny feeling every time I think about it.'

'What sort of feeling? Are you nervous?'

Lisa shook her head. 'Not nervous exactly. Sort of shivery. It's ever since we started the head.'

Fliss laughed. 'You scared of it?'

'Me? No. I don't need to be, Fliss. It's you. You're Ceridwen.'

Fliss pulled a face. 'I know. I had a nightmare. But

26

it's only a story, so there can't really be anything to be afraid of, can there?'

Her friend shrugged. 'I dunno. Maybe not. Anyway, can we talk about something else now, Fliss?'

## CHAPTER SEVEN

Sunday morning was dull and drizzly, but Ellie-May had brought the teeth. Each tooth was twenty centimetres long and came to a good sharp point at one end. Everybody had come in old clothes and they spent a happy hour with the white paint, slapping it on the cones and standing them in a row on Trot's dad's workbench. When the last tooth was done, Trot counted them. 'Twenty-eight,' he said. 'Just right. Seven each side, top and bottom.'

'How do we fix 'em in?' asked Gary.

'Superglue,' Trot told him. 'We gouge out sockets in the papier-mâché, smear 'em with superglue and stick the teeth in. Nothing'll shift 'em once that glue sets. Nothing. But the paint's got to dry first.'

They made the sockets while they were waiting. It wasn't easy. The painted papier-mâché was remarkably tough. By the time they'd finished it was nearly lunchtime and the teeth were almost dry. 'Near enough, anyway,' said Trot, testing one with his finger. 'We can always touch 'em up after if they get fingerprints on 'em.'

By one o'clock the worm's head had a full set of fearsome teeth. The difference was amazing. 'Wow!' breathed Ellie-May. 'Look at it. It's so realistic.'

Trot nodded. 'Sure is. I mean, I know we wanted it scary, but this is almost too frightening. I'd have a fit if I met that in the woods at night.'

'Hey!' Gary's eyes shone. 'Help me on with it – let's see what it looks like moving.'

'No!' Lisa shook her head. 'Don't, Gary. Don't put it on.' She sounded frightened and everybody looked at her.

'What's the matter?' demanded Gary. 'You scared or something?'

Lisa nodded. 'Yes, I'm scared. I don't know why, but I am. It's too good. Too real. I can't believe we made it.'

Trot laughed. 'Who made it if we didn't, Lisa? We're geniuses, kid. It looks good because it was created by a team of brilliant minds. Come on, Gary – let's see our stunning creation in action.'

29

Lisa was backing towards the big double doors. 'I – I've got to go,' she murmured. 'Lunch. I'll see you at school tomorrow, OK?'

'Hey, Lisa.' Fliss looked at her friend. 'Hang on one minute, right? One minute and I'll be with you.'

'No, sorry.' Lisa's face was chalk white. 'I can't. I don't feel well. I have to go now.'

'Oh, all right, I'll come with you.' Fliss shot the others an apologetic glance. 'I'll see you tomorrow.'

When she got outside, Lisa was halfway down the drive. Fliss had to run to catch up. 'You're acting crazy, d'you know that?' she panted. 'They'll drop you from the team if you're not careful.'

'Let them,' said Lisa. 'I'll probably drop out anyway.'

'But why, Lisa? You volunteered for the worm, you know. Nobody forced you.'

'Listen.' Lisa spun on her heel and faced her friend. 'Don't you feel anything when you look at that head? Those teeth? I do. I feel like – like it's all too easy. I mean, that head's perfect, Fliss. Perfect. Stuff you make out of papier-mâché just doesn't turn out like that, especially when a lot of people work on it. You get lumps and dents – it ends up the wrong shape. You know what I mean.'

'Yes.' Fliss nodded. 'We do seem to have been lucky. We slapped the thing together and by sheer chance it came out right. But does that mean we should be scared of it?'

'I'm not scared of it.'

'Well, you could have fooled me. You looked terrified, backing out of that garage. Look.' She put an arm round Lisa and squeezed her skinny waist. 'I'm your friend, right? Whatever's bugging you, you can tell me.'

Lisa nodded. 'I know.' They walked on. 'It's hard to explain, Fliss, but I'm not afraid of the worm. Not in the way you mean, but all the same there's something about it that's not quite right.' She smiled wanly. 'And if I still feel the same when it's finished, I think I'm going to have to drop out.'

'Well,' sighed Fliss, 'It is odd, I suppose, the way everything's come together so perfectly. Anyway, I'm on your side whatever happens. D'you want to meet up after lunch – walk round town or something?'

Lisa nodded. 'OK. Half-two?'

'Half-two, on the corner. I'll wear my new black jeans.'

## CHAPTER EIGHT

'Hey, I like the gear!' cried Lisa. Fliss did a twirl, showing off her black jeans and top, her brand-new trainers.

'You've perked up a bit,' she grinned. 'Must've been hunger.'

Lisa smiled. 'Maybe.' They fell into step, strolling towards the town centre.

'What we gonna do?' asked Lisa.

Fliss shrugged. 'Not a lot. Everything'll be shut, but some of the kids could be around.' She looked sidelong at her friend. 'We might see Trot.'

'Shut up.'

Fliss was partly right. Most places were shut. McDonald's was open though, and they peered through the big window, looking for friends among the diners. There were none. 'We could go in anyway,' suggested Fliss. 'Have coffee and pie or something.'

'Ugh.' Lisa pulled a face. 'Do you mind? I've just eaten about half a cow and a truckful of veg. Haven't you had lunch? You must have a stomach like a Hoover.'

'I thought it'd be something to do, that's all.'

'I'd rather walk on, boring though it is.'

'I'll tell you what.'

'What?'

'It must've been even more boring when it was just a village.'

Lisa looked at her. 'What made you think of that?'

'The play, of course.'

'Hmmm.' Lisa grinned. 'No McDonald's, that's for sure, but they did have the worm to liven things up.'

Fliss giggled. 'D'you reckon it was exciting waiting for it to come out of the marsh, never knowing when it might be your turn to get eaten?'

Lisa shook her head. 'Horrible, I should think. Terrifying. Like a village in India when there's a man-eating tiger about. Not boring though.'

'I think I'd rather be bored.'

Lisa laughed. 'I'd rather be the worm.'

Fliss looked at her. 'Fancy human flesh, do you?'

Lisa chuckled. 'Not the flesh, Fliss. The power.'

'How d'you mean?'

'Well, think about it.' Lisa's eyes gleamed. 'Everyone running, hiding, shaking with terror every time you appeared. You could have anything you wanted – make them do whatever you wanted them to do. What a fantastic feeling that'd be.'

Fliss shook her head. 'I think I'd rather be liked, Lisa.'

Lisa laughed. 'That's the whole point, Fliss – you don't need to be liked if you're feared. If they're all scared stiff of you, they'll fall over each other to be your friend.'

There was a note in Lisa's voice which Fliss had never heard before. She gazed at her friend. 'Sounds like you've thought it all out, Lisa. I never knew stuff like that went on inside your skull.'

Lisa frowned. 'It didn't. Not till this worm thing started. It's doing my head in if you want to know, Fliss. I can't stop thinking about it.'

'Well, if it's bothering you so much, maybe you should drop out, but I don't get it. It's only a play, for Pete's sake, with a papier-mâché monster we made ourselves.' Fliss wished she felt as certain as she sounded.

Lisa nodded. 'I know, and I don't understand either. I—' She broke off, peering along the street

34

they'd just turned into. Some way down, a great yellow skip stood on the pavement. Men were hurrying in and out of a building, throwing things into the skip, going back for more. 'What's going on, Fliss – what place is that?'

Fliss shrugged. 'Demolition, by the look of it. It's the Odeon.' The Odeon was Elsworth's only cinema. 'Come on.' She plucked at Lisa's sleeve. 'Let's watch for a bit. It'll be something to do, if nothing else.'

# CHAPTER NINE

They watched from across the street. Two men brought out rolls of carpet and threw them in the skip. A great battered van came nosing along the street and drew up, blocking their view. They crossed over a bit further along and watched from there. The men were carrying out seats of steel and worn plush. These didn't go into the skip. They were lifted from the men's shoulders by two youths in the back of the van, who stacked them in the cavernous interior. 'Wonder where they're going?' whispered Fliss.

'Another cinema?' suggested Lisa.

When the van was crammed with seats, the two youths jumped down, secured its shutter-door and clambered into the cab. The engine coughed and roared and the van lurched away in a fog of blue exhaust. Three demolition men in vests and jeans stood, hands on hips, watching it leave. As they turned to go back inside, one of them noticed the two girls and called to them. 'Wanna buy a cinema, ladies?'

Lisa shook her head. 'Not today, thanks.'

'How much?' asked Fliss.

'Oh, let me see.' The man pretended to calculate. 'Five quid?'

'Sorry, haven't got it. How about sixty-two pence?'

'No chance. Good, solid building this, shoved up in nineteen thirty-two.'

'No seats in it though,' grinned Fliss.

'Yeah, there is – hundreds yet. And anyway, what d'you expect for five quid?'

'Sixty-two pence,' Fliss reminded.

'Aaa – miser, that's all you are.' He turned to follow his mates inside, muttering, 'Sixty-two pence!' as he went.

'You aren't half cheeky, Fliss,' giggled Lisa.

'No I'm not. He started it.'

'I wonder what he'd have done if you'd pulled a fiver out and said "OK"!'

'Sold it to me, of course.' Fliss chuckled. 'Can you imagine my mum's face if I walked in and said, "Mum, I bought the Odeon."?'

Lisa nodded. 'She'd say, "Well, you can't have

the dirty old thing in your room – you must keep it in the shed." '

The two friends were laughing so much when the man reappeared that he had to whistle piercingly to attract their attention. 'If I can't sell you a picture house, what about a nice bit of dress material?' They looked, and saw that he was carrying a mass of satiny green fabric which lay in shimmering folds across his arms. It was so slippery, and there was so much of it, that he was having to steady it with his chin to stop it toppling forward.

'Hey!' breathed Fliss. 'What is it?'

'Curtain,' the man told her. 'You know – they used to pull it across the screen between films. There's another just like it inside. D'you fancy it?'

'You bet. How much?'

The man laughed. 'I don't want your money, love. Here – take it. It'll only get burned if you don't.'

Fliss started forward, but Lisa's fingers snatched at her sleeve. 'What d'you want with an old curtain, Fliss? Come on – let's go, huh?'

'No.' Fliss freed her arm. 'Don't you see? It's exactly what we need to cover the worm with. It's green, it's shiny and it's very, very long. In other words, it's perfect.' She walked up to the demolition man.

'Watch it, love,' he grinned. 'It's heavy.' He tipped it into her arms, and she staggered under its weight.

Her knees buckled as she bore her prize back to Lisa.

'See?' she beamed. 'What a fantastic stroke of luck.'

Lisa shook her head. 'Not luck, Fliss. Fate.'

'What do you mean, fate? What are you on about, Lisa?'

'Fate is what I'm on about, Fliss. The thing that made the frame perfect and the head perfect and the teeth perfect. The thing that made us walk down here, today of all days, so that you could find a perfect skin for our perfect worm. Don't you see? It's all coming too easily.'

Fliss gazed into her friend's troubled eyes. 'Oh, Lisa – it's a run of luck, that's all. It happens. Are you going to help me carry this, or do I have to cripple myself?'

Lisa shrugged. 'I'll help. You know I will, but I wish we hadn't come this way. I wish the horrid thing was all burned up.'

# CHAPTER TEN

'Wanna buy a powerhouse, ladies?'

She and Fliss were on a street. The man wore jeans and a vest and had perfect teeth. 'How much?' asked Fliss.

'McDonald's,' said the man. 'Shoved up in thirteen ninety-two.'

Fliss laughed. 'What d'you want with a power-house, Lisa? Lisa-pisa monkey-greaser.'

'Not the flesh, Fliss. The power. I've thought it all out.'

'I never knew stuff like that went on inside your skull. It's only papier-mâché.'

'Not to me it isn't. It's too perfect.'

'It's a run of luck, that's all.'

The man whistled shrilly to attract their attention. He was much further away now. 'You want this stuff or not?' He was cradling something in his arms but she couldn't see what it was.

'You bet!' she cried, running towards him. Behind her, Fliss was laughing. Her laughter echoed in the street.

For a long time the distance between the man and herself seemed to stay the same, and then in a moment she was with him. He smiled. Close up, she could see fingerprints on his teeth. 'We can always touch 'em up after,' he said, and she saw he'd turned into Trot. 'Here.' He held out what he was carrying.

Fear seized her. 'What is it?'

'A man–eating tiger. They used to pull it across the screen between films.'

'I – I don't like it.' She tried to back away but her feet wouldn't move.

'You don't need to be liked if you're feared.' He tipped the great, snarling cat into her arms and Lisa woke, screaming.

# CHAPTER ELEVEN

'Are you sure you're all right to go this morning, Lisa?' Mrs Watmough eyed her daughter anxiously. She was pale, and the skin under her eyes looked bruised and puffy.

'Sure I am, Mum. I had a dream, that's all.'

'A nightmare, more like. You haven't screamed in the night like that since you were four.'

'I'm OK, Mum, honestly. I feel fine.' She didn't, but both her parents went out to work and she wasn't going to stay alone in the house all day.

'Well, if you're determined—'

''Bye, Mum.'

Determined. Lisa smiled faintly to herself as she walked down the path. I wish I was determined.

About anything. Confused is what I am. Mixed up. Scared, if you want to know the truth. Something's happening to me and I don't understand what it is, except that it's got something to do with the play. Well – we're due to meet with old Hepworth this aft to discuss progress. Maybe I'll ask to drop out. Dunno what excuse I'll come up with though – can't tell him I'm scared, can I?

Fliss was waiting for her at the top of the school drive. 'Hey, Lisa, you look awful. Is something wrong?'

'No, why should there be?'

Fliss shrugged. 'No reason.' She grinned. 'Anyway, here's Trot. He'll cheer you up.'

'Huh – fat chance.'

'Hi, girls,' Trot greeted. 'Seen Gary?'

They shook their heads. 'We've some good news for you though,' said Fliss.

'Let me guess – the school burned down?'

'No.'

'Old Hepworth's got measles?'

'Shut up and listen, will you? We've found a skin for the worm.'

'No kidding! What's it like?' Fliss described the material. 'Is there enough of it, though?'

Fliss nodded. 'It's a cinema curtain. It's higher than the school and nearly as long. It'd do for two worms.'

'Fantastic. Bring it to the garage tonight. Half-seven?'

'Right.'

Trot turned to Lisa. 'Half-seven OK for you?'

She pulled a face. 'Dunno. I might not come. Mum says I need an early night.'

Trot laughed. 'It's not a party, kid. No crates of booze. No rock band. You can be home by nine if that's what you want.'

'I don't know, Trot. I'll have to see, OK?' A part of her wanted to be there. The part that liked to be with Trot. But then there was that other part – the voice inside her head which was telling her to pull back – and that voice was growing louder.

'Sure.' Trot shrugged and went off in search of Gary.

Fliss looked at her friend. 'Are you sure there's nothing you want to talk about, Lisa?'

'I'm sure.' She sighed. 'Look, Fliss, I had a nightmare and I'm tired and I've got things to think about, so d'you think you could just leave me alone for a while, huh?'

'Sure.' Fliss felt hurt. 'I'll leave you alone. I'll stop talking to you altogether, if that's what you want.' She spun on her heel and hurried on down the drive.

# CHAPTER TWELVE

'Right!' Mr Hepworth rubbed his hands together and beamed at Year Eight. 'It's just a week now since Mrs Evans and I sprang on you the task of producing a play for the Festival, and we thought this might be a good time for people to report back on how things are progressing. Not to us – we're here in an advisory capacity only – but to one another. Now – who'd like to kick us off?'

'I'd like to kick you off a cliff,' whispered one of the boys. His friend giggled.

Mr Hepworth glared at them. 'Did you speak, Roger?'

'No, Sir.'

'Then it was you, Michael. What did you say?'

'I – I said I'd like to kick us off, Sir.'

'Splendid – off you go, then.'

'Well, er – I'm a villager, Sir.'

'Yes?'

'And – my mum's nearly finished my outfit. She's made it out of sacking, and it's this raggedy old jacket thing with a belt and some really baggy trousers.'

'In other words, Michael, you'll be dressed much as usual.' Everybody laughed. 'And you, Roger – what are you up to?'

'I'm a Viking, Sir. I can sew a bit so I've done my own costume. Well – my mum helped a bit. And I've made this really wicked helmet, Sir, with wings on it.'

The teacher sighed. 'There's absolutely no evidence that the Vikings wore winged helmets, Roger. It's a fallacy.'

'No, it's a helmet, Sir, honest.'

'Yes, all right, Roger.' Mr Hepworth sounded tired. 'Sarah-Jane – you're the producer or director or whatever, aren't you?'

'Yes, Sir.'

'So how's it coming along?'

'Well – we thought about speaking parts, but in the end we decided to have a narrator because nobody knows how people spoke in those days.'

Mrs Evans nodded. 'Good idea, Sarah-Jane. Who's narrating?'

Andrew Roberts raised his hand. 'Me, Miss.'

Mrs Evans nodded. 'I can't say I'm surprised, Andrew. You've spent most of your time in this school narrating when you should have been listening. Go on, Sarah-Jane.'

'We've had a couple of rehearsals, Miss. Well – not really rehearsals. Trying things out, and it seems OK so far. We don't have people's costumes at school, and of course the worm's not ready, but—'

'It nearly is,' interrupted Trot. 'We've got everything. Now all we have to do is fit the skin and figure out a way to make it breathe fire.'

'Just a minute, David.' Mr Hepworth smiled. 'I know we want this worm to look as realistic as possible, but I think we're going to have to draw the line at fire-breathing.'

'Aw, Sir—?'

'No, David, I'm sorry. Anything you could devise would be highly dangerous. Just think what would happen if the worm caught fire with people inside it. It might be possible to fake smoke using dry ice or something, but there's to be no fire. Is that understood?'

'Yes, Sir.' Trot looked crestfallen.

'I thought he was here in an advisory capacity,' hissed Neil Atkinson.

The teacher looked up sharply. 'He is, and he has sharp ears, and his advice to you is to keep

comments of that sort to yourself. All right?'
'Yes, Sir.'

From the start of the session, Lisa had struggled silently with herself. A part of her wanted to withdraw from the play, or at least from the worm, while another part – a dark, submerged part of herself whose existence she hadn't even suspected a week ago – urged her in excited whispers to say nothing: to hold on to her place inside the worm and see where it might lead her. And this had nothing to do with Trot. She was fond of him, of course, but this was something else; something altogether darker, more compelling. And the dark part won. When twenty to three rolled round and the teachers brought the session to an end, she'd said nothing.

I'll do it, she cried inwardly, and a tingle ran down her spine into her tummy-muscles. When Fliss approached her gingerly at home-time she seemed her old self, and they chatted as they dawdled up the drive. Only Lisa knew she'd given in to something dark and strong, and neither girl knew their paths were set to diverge, or that when they came together again it would be as enemies.

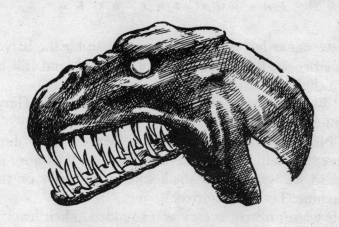

## CHAPTER THIRTEEN

When Fliss got to Trot's at twenty-five past seven, Lisa was already there. Fliss's arms ached from carrying the curtain. She let it fall to the floor. Ellie-May and the two boys went down on their knees to look and feel. 'It's terrific, Fliss!' cried Gary.

Ellie-May lifted a fold, rubbed it against her cheek and let it slip through her fingers. 'Yeah, terrific. It's shiny, like it might be covered with slime or something, and the colour's exactly right. How long is it?'

They measured, and the curtain proved to be more than ten metres long. Lisa pulled a face. 'Pity. The real worm was twice as long.'

'Yes,' said Fliss, 'but remember it's very wide.

49

If we cut it in two lengthways and stitch the halves together we'll still have plenty of width and it'll be just the right length.'

'Who's going to do all this stitching?' asked Gary. 'I'm useless at sewing.'

'No problem,' Trot told him. 'My mum's volunteered to help. All we have to do is tack it more or less as we want it and she'll stitch it properly on the machine. Let's get started.'

It wasn't nearly as easy as it sounded. Their lengthways cut was a bit wavy and it took ages to fasten the two pieces together, even with Trot's big tacking stitch. Then they had to drape the slippery material over the worm's neck and body and mark where they'd attach the tapes which would be knotted under the worm's belly to fasten the skin to the frame. When that was done, they spread the fabric on the floor and took turns sewing on the tapes in such a way that they wouldn't be visible to an audience. It was twenty past nine by the time they'd finished, and they'd done nothing with the fifteen metres of material which would form the monster's tail. 'Leave that,' said Trot. 'My mum's clever. She'll figure out a way to cut and stitch so it tapers to a nice sharp tip.'

'Let's try it out,' suggested Gary. 'Fliss can tie the tapes, and the end can just trail for now like a peacock's tail. What d'you say?'

'I say yes!' cried Lisa, eyes shining.

'OK,' said Trot, 'only don't step on the tail or it'll rip off and all my brill tacking will go to waste.' He turned to Fliss. 'Will you do the tapes?'

Fliss shrugged. 'Sure, but don't be too long, OK? I was supposed to be home for half-nine.'

The four stood in line and lowered the frame over their heads while Fliss held the skin to stop it sliding off the hoops. Yells and laughs came from inside the worm as Fliss knelt, pulling down on the tapes and tying them. 'Hey, it's dark in here!' complained Ellie-May. 'I can't see where I'm going.'

I can see for all of us,' said Gary from the front. 'Put your hands on Trot's shoulders, Ellie-May, and go where he goes. Trot puts his on Lisa's and Lisa has hers on mine. Easy-peasy.'

It wasn't easy. Not at first, within the confines of the Trotter family's garage. Peering through the eye-holes on the worm's neck, Gary went off at a slow walk, twisting and turning to avoid walls, worktops and obstructions on the floor. The others followed as best they could, with frequent exclamations and much giggling. Fliss leaned against the workbench and watched. She wished they'd stop now so she could undo the tapes and go home, but they didn't.

At twenty to ten, Gary broke into a slow trot and the others followed suit. The worm danced sinuously through the darkening garage, its great

51

head swaying and bobbing. Now and then its reflector eyes would catch light from somewhere and flash red. Fliss was amazed at the dexterity of her friends; their co-ordination. The way their dancing feet avoided the great train of fabric they trailed, which slid, hissing, across the dusty concrete. The ease with which they seemed to have mastered the technique. Their shouts of laughter grew louder as Gary increased his speed, but there were no disasters – nobody stumbled. Fliss watched as though mesmerized, and when she remembered to look at her watch it was ten to ten.

'Hey!' Their exultant laughter drowned her voice. 'Hey, you guys. It's almost ten. I've got to go.'

Nobody heard. Gary shifted up another gear and they came whooping in his wake, precisely, like a well-drilled squad. Fliss moved over to the wall switch and snapped on the lights. At once and in unison the dancers broke into a rhythmic chant of 'Off, off, off!'

Fliss shook her head. 'No – it's ten o'clock.'

'You what?' cried Gary, and the others took it up: 'You what, you what, you what?'

'I have to go.' She was close to tears.

'Go, go, go!'

'Lisa?' Surely her best friend would respond – break step so that the dance could end in red-faced, panting laughter?

'Lisa?' they mimicked, and her voice was among

52

them. 'Lisa, Lisa, Lisa, Lisa, Lisa—' The worm was coming at her now, eyes burning, jaws agape.

She turned and fled.

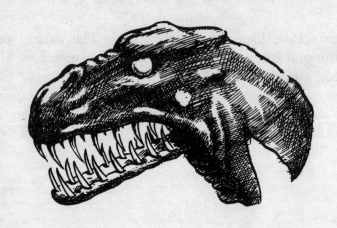

## CHAPTER FOURTEEN

'Ceridwen, Ceridwen.' Mockery in their eyes, their voices.

'The worm. Terrific skin.'

'Triffic, triffic, triffic.'

'Tied with tapes.'

'Tape-worm, then. Heeee!'

'People inside, see?'

'Room for another though.'

'Room for one inside.'

'You, Ceridwen. Room for you.'

'I'm not Ceridwen!' she screamed. 'I'm Fliss.'

'Fliss!' they cried. 'Flass, Fluss, Floss.' Pressing in, crowding her so that she was forced to move out to where the worm danced. There it was. Its red, mad

54

eyes and pinky, fang-crammed maw. It saw her and came slithering on a zig-zag path towards her. She tried to throw herself back, but they caught her and flung her forward again. The worm was close now. So close she could smell the putrid stench of its breath. Its slavering jaws gaped to engulf her. 'Room for one inside.' The voice was Gary's.

Fliss woke, damp and shaking. It was a long time before she slept again.

## CHAPTER FIFTEEN

Tuesday morning. For the first time ever, Fliss didn't want to meet Lisa at the end of the road for the walk to school. She dawdled so long over breakfast that her mother started giving her funny looks. 'Fliss,' she said. 'Are you feeling all right?'

'I'm fine, Mum.' Pushing Coco Pops round her bowl.

'Then eat your breakfast, dear. It's almost twenty to nine. Lisa will go without you.'

That's the general idea, she thought, but didn't say. Her mother dropped toast on her plate. Fliss pushed aside the unfinished cereal and began to butter a slice as carefully as if she were painting a masterpiece. Her mother sighed, cleared Dad's place and ran water into the sink.

Fliss knew her tactic had failed the moment she turned out of the driveway. The end of the road was about a hundred metres away and Lisa was there, waiting. It was almost ten to nine, for Pete's sake. They'd practically have to run to reach school on time, yet there she was. Fliss thought of ducking back into the driveway but if she did she'd certainly be late for school, and anyway Lisa had probably spotted her. With a grimace of resignation she walked towards the girl she'd regarded till lately as her best friend.

'Hi, Fliss. Why d'you leave in such a rush last night?' Lisa sounded genuinely concerned.

Fliss gazed at her. 'Are you kidding? After the way you all ignored me and mocked me and then came at me as though you meant to trample me into the floor? You'd have left in a rush too. Anyone would.'

'Would I heck!' Lisa's tone was scornful. 'It was a bit of fun, that's all.'

'Well, it wasn't fun for me, Lisa. It scared me, the way the four of you moved in that thing as though—'

'As though we'd been doing it all our lives,' finished Lisa. 'That's what you were going to say, isn't it?'

Fliss nodded. 'Something like that, yes.'

'And that's exactly how it felt, Fliss.' Lisa's eyes

57

shone. 'We couldn't put a foot wrong, any of us. I mean, you'd think— I expected we'd stumble and fumble around, you know? Knock things over, step on our own tail, fall down. Three of us couldn't even see, and yet we ended up running, Fliss. Running like one creature, not four. I can't describe the feeling except to say it was awesome. Sincerely awesome.'

'Yes, well, like I said, it was no fun for me.'

Lisa laughed. 'You shouldn't have joined if you can't take a joke, Fliss. And anyway, you'll get the last laugh, won't you?'

'How d'you mean?'

'You're Ceridwen, aren't you? Heroine-Saint of Elsworth? You get to vanquish the worm, remember?'

'Oh, yes. I see what you mean, but I still don't like the way you ganged up with the others against me last night, Lisa. You're supposed to be my friend.'

Lisa sighed. 'I am your friend, Fliss. Same as always, only you're not in the worm, see? You don't know what it's like 'cause you're not part of it, and that's bound to make a difference, right?'

Fliss shook her head. 'I don't see why. It's only a play when all's said and done.'

'Ah, but is it?'

'What d'you mean? Of course it is.'

'I dunno – maybe it is, maybe it isn't. Inside that worm last night it felt like something bigger, Fliss. Much bigger.'

'I don't know what you're talking about, Lisa. You've been talking crazy-talk ever since this play thing started and I wish you wouldn't. It scares me. I'll be glad when the Festival's over and the worm's gone for good.'

'If.'

'Huh?'

'If, not when. How do you know the worm'll go? It might win this time.'

'Don't be daft.'

Lisa shrugged. 'OK.' She looked at her watch. 'Two minutes to nine. Last one in school's a creepazoid.' She broke into a run and Fliss followed, wondering what old Hepworth would say when she told him she wasn't going to play Ceridwen.

# CHAPTER SIXTEEN

The plate on the door said 'Deputy Head'. Fliss knocked. 'Come in.' She pushed open the door. Mr Hepworth smiled from the swivel chair behind his cluttered desk. 'Now then, Felicity, what can we do for you?'

'I don't want to be Ceridwen in the play, Sir.'

'Why ever not?'

'I don't really know, Sir. I mean, I know it sounds daft but I had this dream. This nightmare, about the worm. It scared me. And then last night—'

'What about last night?'

'Well, I don't want to get anybody into trouble, Sir, but something happened last night at David Trotter's and that scared me too.'

Mr Hepworth leaned forward across the desk. 'What sort of something, Felicity?'

'The worm, Sir. We finished the worm and they got inside it and—'

'Who? Who got inside it?'

'Ellie-May Sunderland, David Trotter, Gary Bazzard and Lisa Watmough, Sir. They're playing the worm.'

'I see. Go on.'

Fliss related the evening's events, including her flight from the garage. When she'd finished, the Deputy Head nodded. 'I can see how a thing like that might upset you, Felicity, but I'm not altogether surprised that it happened, considering who was in control of the worm.' He sighed. 'Whatever possessed Year Eight to put Gary Bazzard in the worm's head?'

'Well, he wanted to be the Viking Chief, Sir, but we'd decided to have a girl for that part, so Gary got the worm's head as a sort of consolation.'

'Well, it's Year Eight's production and we promised not to interfere, but I have to say that Mrs Evans and I probably would not have set our hearts on consoling Gary Bazzard, Felicity. The class gives him a leading role and he shows his gratitude by intimidating you with what sounds like a typical display of hooliganism. That's the sort of lad he is, I'm afraid.'

Fliss shook her head. 'It's not that that bothers

me, Sir. Gary's all mouth. I can cope with him any time. It's – other things that have happened. Things that have been said.'

Mr Hepworth shook his head. 'You're going to have to explain that, Felicity. You've lost me somewhere along the line.'

Fliss tried, but the things she had to say sounded ridiculous even to her, in the Deputy Head's office in broad daylight. The way they'd found everything they needed to make the worm. Lisa's remarks about fate. How the creature had turned out perfect without any striving on the part of its makers, and how easily the four children had learned to work it, as though they'd been doing it all their lives. And the change which seemed to have come over Lisa since she'd become involved. It was worrying stuff when you put it together but she spoke stumblingly and with-out conviction, presenting the teacher with a hopeless jumble of suppositions. When her voice tailed off in mid-sentence, he smiled.

'It's up to you, Felicity, but if you want my opinion it's this. Both you and Lisa Watmough have highly developed imaginations, and you've allowed them to run away with you a little. This, coupled with Gary Bazzard's typically idiotic antic, has given rise to needless anxiety on your part, the upshot of which is that you now wish to relinquish your part in the play.' He smiled again and shook his head. 'I don't think you should do that, Felicity. I feel you'd regret it later, when Year Eight's production turns out to be the highlight of the Festival. No. If I were you I'd be inclined to carry on. Put a bit of a curb on that imagination of yours, and remember that life is full of coincidences which may seem to add up to more than coincidence when you get a string of them together. And if I were producing this play, which I'm not, I'd stick Richard Varley in the worm's head and demote young Bazzard to understudy.' He arched his brow. 'All right, Felicity?'

Fliss nodded, looking into her lap. She wasn't convinced, not really. But she'd failed to convince the teacher so perhaps he was right. It did all seem a bit far-fetched now. Very far-fetched, in fact. She looked up. 'I'll try, Sir,' she said.

## CHAPTER SEVENTEEN

She hadn't long to wait. While she'd been seeing the Deputy Head at morning break, Trot and Gary had collared Sarah-Jane and told her Trot's mum was finishing the skin, and that the worm would be complete by midday. Sarah-Jane persuaded them to go and fetch it in their lunch break so they could have a run-through with it. Then she went along to the staffroom and persuaded Mrs Evans to release Year Eight from English that afternoon for a rehearsal.

When Mrs Trotter's car pulled into the parking lot at ten past one that day, a crowd gathered to watch Trot and Gary unload their creation. It was in three separate pieces, but one of those pieces – the papier-mâché head and neck – was impressive enough to draw gasps and whistles from the watchers. 'Woweee!' cried a first-year kid. 'Look at it – it's so real, like they chopped the head off an actual dragon.'

'Yeah,' breathed another. 'And look at the eyes, man. They stare at you, don't they? I reckon they can see.'

A posse of kids trailed after the two boys as they lugged their burden up the steps. They'd have followed right into school if two prefects hadn't been guarding the door. Trot and Gary were stowing the worm in the Year Eight stockroom when Mrs Evans came in. 'So this is it, eh?' She gazed at the head. 'Ugh!' She shivered. 'I wouldn't want to meet that on a dark night, David. Did you do all this yourselves?'

'Yes, Miss.'

'Well, you've made a really good job of it, I'll give you that. Papier-mâché isn't the easiest stuff to work with, and those eyes are most effective. What are they?'

'Car reflectors, Miss.'

'Car reflectors. Yes. Well – I can't wait to see the creature in action.' She smiled. 'Well done.'

'Ta, Miss.'

'Ta?' Mrs Evans shot Gary a disapproving look. 'Surely you mean "Thank you, Miss"?'

'Oh – yeah. Thank you, Miss.'

'Hmmm.'

As Mrs Evans left the room, Mr Hepworth stuck his head round the door. 'What's this I hear about a monster?' His eyes fell on the head. 'Good heavens.' He came forward, stretching out a hand to touch its glossy skin. 'You've done a remarkable job here, lads. I don't wonder young Felicity had a nightmare.'

'Did she, Sir?' Gary's face was all sweet innocence.

The teacher looked at him. 'Yes, Gary Bazzard, she did, and if I hear of any more hooliganism on your part, you'll be out. Not only out of the worm but out of the play completely. I'd have thought by Year Eight you'd have grown out of that silly behaviour.'

'What silly behaviour, Sir? I don't know what you mean.'

'Yes you do, and it's got to stop. As of now. Understand?'

'Yessir.'

Mr Hepworth departed and they finished stowing the worm. As Trot closed the stockroom door, Gary spoke softly. 'There's a snitch in our midst, Trot. A tattletale.'

Trot nodded. 'Sounds like it. What we gonna do?'

'Oh, I dunno, Trot. I'll think of something.' Gary smiled. 'Something messy, I shouldn't wonder.'

# CHAPTER EIGHTEEN

The hall was in use for PE, so they had to use Mrs Evans's room for the tryout. She supervised the stacking of chairs and tables along one wall to make floorspace, then disappeared in the direction of the staffroom with a pile of marking.

'Right.' Sarah-Jane perched herself on a window-ledge to do her producer bit. 'How are costumes coming along?'

'Mine's ready,' said Gemma, 'but it's at home.'

Fliss nodded. 'Mine too. Nobody said we were rehearsing today.'

'I know,' grinned Sarah-Jane. 'It was a spur of the moment decision. I couldn't wait to see the worm in action. Has anybody brought their costume?'

Nobody had, but it didn't really matter. The only costume anybody was interested in at the moment lay in three pieces in the Year Eight stockroom. Trot and Gary carted it out and there was no shortage of volunteers to help Ellie-May, Lisa and the two boys into it. When the last tape was tied, Gary led his team on a trial circuit of the classroom under the admiring gaze of their classmates. Mrs Trotter had stuffed and sewn the long tail beautifully. It was rounded and tapered and flexible and it looped and snaked across the floor as the monster circled.

'OK,' said Sarah-Jane, when the worm had done three circuits. 'That's beautiful, but I got us off English and we're supposed to be working.'

'Let's do the bits where the worm seizes villagers and drags them off,' suggested Keith.

There was a general cry of 'Yeah!' and Sarah-Jane nodded, pointing. 'That's the village, over in that corner. Get over there if you're a villager.'

'Which bit's Norway?' demanded Barry Tune. Sarah-Jane looked at him. 'What d'you mean, which bit's Norway? What's Norway got to do with it?'

'That's where the Vikings were when the worm was eating peopleburgers,' said Barry. 'So that's where us Vikings should stand.'

'Don't be daft,' snapped Sarah-Jane. 'The Vikings aren't in this bit. They can stand round the walls and watch.'

68

'Boring,' muttered Barry. 'If there's one thing a Viking hates, it's being bored.' Some of the other Vikings muttered their agreement. Sarah-Jane ignored them. Meanwhile the villagers had crammed themselves into their corner and were arguing over who should be the first victim, while the worm glared balefully at them through its mad red eyes.

After some pushing and shoving, Tara Matejak was thrust forward by Michael who cried, 'Here's your starter, worm.'

'Just a minute!' Gary, who was moving towards the girl, stopped at the sound of Sarah-Jane's voice. Sarah-Jane glared at Michael. 'Is that what you intend saying on the day, Michael Tostevin?'

The boy grinned. ''Course not.'

'Then don't say it in rehearsal, OK?'

Michael shrugged. 'OK, Miss. Sorry, Miss.' Some of his friends tittered.

Sarah-Jane sighed. 'OK, worm – carry on.'

When it came to it, the business of seizing and dragging off proved far more difficult than anyone had envisaged. The jaws of the monster were not a moving part. They were set permanently agape and could seize nothing, so that Tara had to co-operate in her own abduction, thrusting her hand into a corner of the worm's mouth and walking beside it in such a way as to suggest that she was being dragged by the arm. It wasn't completely successful, and Trot undertook to devise a way of enabling the beast to grab its living meals more convincingly in future.

Fliss observed all of this with apprehension, praying that time would run out before Sarah-Jane decided enough villagers had perished and called upon Ceridwen to confront the worm. She'd promised Mr Hepworth she'd try, but her classmates' dexterity inside that awful disguise disturbed her even here, and she was far from happy. It must have been her lucky day, because the buzzer went as the beast prepared to bear away its sixth victim.

'OK.' Sarah-Jane slid down from her perch. 'Wrap it up, everybody.' She smiled. 'That wasn't bad, but I want all costumes in school tomorrow.' She turned to Trot, who was struggling out of his disguise like a moth from a chrysalis. 'Don't forget, Trot – the worm needs to be able to grab its prey.'

Trot nodded. 'I'll think of something.'

Sarah-Jane turned to speak to Fliss, and was mildly irritated to find she was no longer in the room.

# CHAPTER NINETEEN

She was passing the Deputy Head's office on her way out when the door opened. 'Ah, Felicity, come in a minute, will you?' Mr Hepworth stepped to one side and she went in. He closed the door and stood with his back to it. 'Now – how did the rehearsal go?'

'All right, Sir.'

'No trouble from our friend Mr Bazzard?'

'No, Sir.'

'Good. I had a word with him and it seems to have worked. So, are you feeling a bit happier about things now, Felicity? We wouldn't want to lose your talents, you know.'

Happier? Fliss would have laughed out loud if she'd dared. Mr Hepworth had had a word with

Gary, which meant Gary knew she'd complained. He'd have her marked down as a sneak. He'd tell the others. Her name would be mud.

'I – dunno. Sir. We didn't get to my part. I'll try.'

'Good girl.' He opened the door. 'Off you go, then. And let me know if you have any more hassle.'

'Yessir. G'night, Sir.'

'Goodbye, Felicity.'

'Let me know if you have any more hassle.' That's a laugh for a start, she thought. I can tell you now there'll be hassle, but there's no way I'm gonna let you know. No way.

The drive was thick with pupils going home. Fliss dodged between them, hurrying, looking for Lisa. Lisa knows how these things happen, she thought. She'll understand. I'll tell her I didn't mean to get anybody into trouble. It just came out.

She was through the gateway and well along the road before she spotted her friend. Lisa was walking with Ellie-May Sunderland. They were dawdling, deep in conversation. Fliss put on a spurt and caught up. 'Hi, Lisa, Ellie-May.'

The two girls regarded her coldly. 'What do you want?' asked Lisa.

'I've got something to tell you.'

'We're talking. See you tomorrow, OK?'

'What's up – what have I done?'

'You know.'

'No I don't.'

'You split on us to old Hepworth.'

'No I didn't. Not on purpose. That's what I wanted to talk to you about.'

'We're not interested in excuses, Fliss. You split on us. That's all that matters.'

'Yes, but—'

'No buts.'

'Are you out tonight, then? We could—'

'No. We're busy tonight, working on the worm.'

'I'll come to Trot's then, shall I?'

Lisa laughed. 'I wouldn't if I were you, Fliss.'

'What d'you mean?'

'What d'you think I mean? Gary's after you, dummy. He'd love you to show up at Trot's. You'd come on foot and leave in an ambulance.'

'But what about you, Lisa? You're not Gary. You don't have to do everything he does. We're friends, aren't we?'

'No, Fliss, we're not, since you ask. Why don't you get lost and leave us in peace?'

'I—' Fliss realized with horror that she was about to cry. Biting her lip she turned away and crossed the road, half-blind with tears. There was an entry – a narrow walkway between two buildings which led on to waste ground. She turned into it, away from the stream of chattering kids, and when she was alone, she wept.

That night, Fliss dreamed again. She'd grown since her bridesmaid day. The long white dress no longer covered her ankles, so Mum had let down the hem to lengthen it. Now she wanted Fliss to try it on, but the alteration had transformed the dress. Mum couldn't see it – she was holding the thing out for her to slip into – but it wasn't a dress any more. It was a—

'A shroud!' She was screaming, shaking her head. 'Can't you see, Mum? It's a shroud.'

'Don't be silly, dear. Come – try it on.' Mum advanced on her, smiling.

'No.' Backing away, hands out to ward off the loathsome garment. Bitter tang of tears in her mouth. Backing towards the door, which opened. Mr Hepworth came in, smiling. 'Try, Fliss,' he crooned. 'Try it on. It is like a shroud, but life is full of coincidences.'

'No, I don't want to. Leave me alone.'

'Typically idiotic antic.'

They rushed, seized her. She struggled, but the Deputy Head was holding her from behind and Mum had the cold fabric over her head. It clung, reeking of sodden clay, smothering her. She jerked herself this way and that. Couldn't breathe. Dark rising. Can't breathe can't breathe can't breathe —

She woke with her face pressed in the pillow and the bedclothes on the floor.

# CHAPTER TWENTY

Ronnie Millhouse was the town drunk. Everybody knew him by sight – he was what is known as a 'character' – but nobody knew the trouble he'd seen. Like all drunks he'd once had an ordinary life, but then the trouble had struck and he'd taken to the lotion in a big way. Now he spent his days on the street, cadging ten and twenty pence pieces from passers-by. 'Have you got any spare change?' he'd ask. 'A few pence for a cup of tea?' People either brushed past him looking angry, or fished in their pockets looking embarrassed, and most days there were enough of the latter sort to provide poor Ronnie with the price of several cups of tea. He didn't waste it on tea, of course. Ronnie's refreshment usually came in a fat brown bottle with a picture of a woodpecker on it. At night, when the wind blew chill and the stream of passers-by dried to a trickle, Ronnie would make his way to the derelict bandstand in the park, where he had a cardboard box for an hotel and a drift of old newspapers for his bed.

At eleven-thirty that Tuesday night, while Fliss lay dreaming, Ronnie was shuffling unsteadily along the footpath which led to the bandstand. A fine drizzle was falling. On his left was the kiddies' playground where the swings hung motionless on dripping chains and the slide gleamed wetly in the light from a distant streetlamp. To his right, the ground fell away in a long slope, thickly planted with trees and shrubs. At the foot of this slope, hidden even in daylight by the trees, was a stretch of level grassland on which, from time to time in the summer months, funfairs and circuses would pitch their camps. Now, as he headed for his bed at the end of a better-than-average day, Ronnie thought he heard voices on the slope. Now Ronnie was a cautious man even when drunk, and he knew there was a better-than-even chance that anybody you'd meet in a public park late at night would be up to no good, so he swerved off the path and pressed himself up against the wet trunk of a thickish tree to see who might appear.

There was a scraping, crackling sound like something big in the shrubbery. Whatever it was, was coming up the slope pretty fast. Ronnie pressed himself more closely to his tree and peeped round, and it was then he saw the dragon. He screwed up his eyes and shook his head and looked again but it was still there, coming off the slope on to the footpath. Its teeth gleamed white and its eyes blazed red. He couldn't make out its colour in the dark, but as it crossed the path and headed for the playground he saw that it was incredibly long. He stood absolutely still and held his breath as the monster's whiplike tail hissed across the tarmac. He hugged his tree while the great shape crossed the playground, nor did he stir for some time after darkness swallowed the beast and all was quiet.

When Ronnie finally let go of the tree and resumed his journey it was twenty minutes before midnight. Half a mile away, Fliss had just woken from her nightmare. It was still drizzling.

Ronnie reached the bandstand and got into bed. He lay on the dusty boards and thought about the dragon. For a while he told himself he'd report what he'd seen. He'd tell the police or the local paper. His fuddled brain created a fantasy in which for once, people were interested in him. A fantasy in which he was somebody because of what he had seen.

It soon faded though. He'd had a good day. A two-bottle day. Who needs fame when there are bottles waiting to be drained? And what's a dragon, compared to some of the creatures Ronnie

Millhouse had seen? Pink lizards. That kangaroo in pinstripe suit and bowler who'd tipped him a fiver. The bright green ants who sometimes ate his hands. No. He'd not tell. Why should he? Waste of time.

Drizzle fell endlessly. Wind lifted a corner of his paper blanket. Ronnie Millhouse slept.

# CHAPTER TWENTY-ONE

'Morning, Mum, Dad.'

Lisa sat down, reached for the packet and sprinkled cornflakes in her bowl. She'd overslept. Dad was halfway down his second cup of coffee and Mum had had to call her twice. She avoided their eyes, hoping they'd say nothing, but it was a forlorn hope.

'Tired, are we?' her father enquired.

'She ought to be,' said her mother, 'coming in at midnight, bold as brass, saying she's been busy. I'll give her busy if it ever happens again.'

Her husband nodded. 'Where was she, that's what I'd like to know.'

Lisa sighed. She hated it when her parents discussed her as if she wasn't there and besides, they'd been over all this last night. 'I told you,' she mumbled. 'I was at David Trotter's, working on the worm.'

'Till midnight?'

'Yes, Mum. It was a big job.'

'It must have been. I'm surprised at the Trotters, letting kids your age stay out till that time. Didn't they realize we'd worry?'

Lisa shook her head. 'They were out, Mum. I told you.'

'We know what you told us, young woman,' rapped her father, 'and now I'll tell *you* something. If anything of this sort happens again I'll be along to school to see Mr Hepworth, and we'll have you out of that play. I'm not having a daughter of mine staying out all night at thirteen years of age, no matter how busy she is. Do you understand?'

'Yes, Dad.'

'Well, I certainly hope so. And I hope you can attend to your lessons today without falling asleep at your desk.'

It was nearly ten to nine when Lisa finally got out of the house. It was still raining, and she wasn't surprised to find no Fliss waiting at the end of the road. She wasn't surprised, and she didn't care. She didn't want to talk to Fliss. It would be no use talking to her. Fliss didn't know. She hadn't been there. You had to have been there to know how it felt, running through the dark. The dark in the park. She smiled briefly at the unintentional rhyme. The park after dark, where you'd hardly dare venture in ordinary circumstances because of the hooligans and the glue-sniffers and the funny men Mum was always on about. You'd stay away if you'd any sense, unless you were part of the worm.

Part of the worm! She laughed out loud, remembering. What a fantastic feeling, running through the dark, fearless because you are part of the most fearsome thing in the park. Fearless because nothing exists which can harm you. There is nothing which wouldn't run screaming and blubbering at your approach. Hooligans, glue-sniffers, funny men. All fleeing, fleeing before – before ME! Lisa's exultant laugh turned a few heads among early shoppers as she ran with her head thrown back and her hair flying, to recapture a scrap of last night's fierce, narcotic joy.

# CHAPTER TWENTY-TWO

'"The time – a little over one thousand years ago. The place – Elsworth, then a mere village, set in the midst of —"'

'Can't hear him!'

'Speak up, you mumbling creepazoid!'

'OK, you lot, you've made your point.' Sarah-Jane looked across the field to where Andrew Roberts stood between the goal-posts, clutching his script. 'You'll have to project a bit, Andrew. Remember we're outside and there's a bit of a breeze.'

The narrator nodded. 'Shall I start again, then?'

'Please.'

It was lunchtime. Year Eight, resplendent in full costume, were rehearsing on the school playing field before a packed audience. It had stopped raining only an hour before and the grass was wet, but Sarah-Jane had been determined and so here they were, Vikings and villagers, saint and serpent, in full regalia, hoping to get through the whole thing before the bell.

' "The time – a little over one thousand years ago. The place – Elsworth, then a mere village, set in the midst of misty fenland. Elsworth, a once quiet village where terror now reigns, for the nearby fen has become the dwelling-place of a monster – a monster known to every terrified inhabitant as THE WORM." '

Behind the narrator and his goal-posts, the field fell away in a steep grassy bank to the stone wall which at this side marked the boundary of school property. After rain, the strip of land between the foot of the bank and the wall became waterlogged, forming a moat of brown water and sticky mud. As Andrew spoke the worm appeared, lurching up the bank to the cheers and whistles of the watching multitude before trotting the length of the field on eight muddy feet to assault the goal-mouth at that end, which was crammed with villagers. This time, Joanne O'Connor was selected as the creature's first victim and pushed out towards the penalty spot. The worm ran at the girl as if it meant to boot her into the back of the net, but at the last moment Gary reached out

83

and grabbed her. The crowd roared, drowning Joanne's half-genuine scream as she was hustled over the halfway line with her feet off the ground.

'Right!' Sarah-Jane flapped a hand at the worm. 'You can put her down now, Gary – we get the idea. Brilliant solution by the way, but time's short. Can we go to Ceridwen please?'

Fliss, who'd been standing on the touchline trying to keep the hem of her dress clear of the mud, felt her heart kick. She'd known this moment would come, but had expected Sarah-Jane to allow the worm a few more victims before calling on her. She caught her bottom lip between her teeth and stepped forward, holding a plastic sword, hoping nobody would notice her nervousness.

'Gary.' Sarah-Jane gestured towards the banking from which the worm had made its entrance. 'Out of sight, please. Fliss – you walk out of the village while Andrew's doing his next bit and stand on the halfway line. When the worm rushes you, raise your sword as if you're going to slash at its neck. Gary.' The worm paused, seeming to glare at the director with its mad eyes. 'You shoot out your arms to grab her like you did with Joanne, but as soon as your hand brushes the dress you back off, looking submissive. Can you do that?' The worm made no reply, but turned and loped off towards the banking. When it was out of sight, Sarah-Jane nodded to the narrator, who began to speak. Fliss swallowed hard and set off for the middle of the field.

' "—armed only with a short sword and her faith, stood directly in its path." ' Andrew stopped speaking. The worm topped the rise to the cheers of the spectators and came trotting towards Fliss, its great head swaying from side to side. Fliss swallowed again, gripped her sword tightly and lifted it above her head.

That's when it all went wrong. Gary's arms appeared, but he didn't brush the dress. Instead, he grabbed her on the run and turned, and Fliss found herself being carried swiftly back the way the worm had come. She kicked and shouted and laid about her with the sword but it was no use. Gary's hold was like the hug of a bear. Ignoring Sarah-Jane's cries, he carried Fliss to the top of the slope, hissed, 'Tattletale!' through the eye-holes and flung her down. Helpless, she half rolled, half skidded down the banking and into the moat. The crowd, believing this to be part of the show, cheered themselves hoarse as she lay winded, feeling the spread of clammy wetness which would turn the white dress brown.

# CHAPTER TWENTY-THREE

The show had to go on, and the Vikings were
making their first raid as Fliss picked herself up
and ran sobbing to the girls' changing-room. She
pulled off the sodden dress and held it up. It was
so obviously ruined that she flung it to the floor and
flopped down on a bench, weeping. Her first thought
was, Right – that's it. I'm out. As soon as I get cleaned
up, I'm off to Hepworth to tell him I'm not doing it.
She stripped for the shower, and as she stood under
the warm torrent it occurred to her that Gary and the
others might actually be trying to get rid of her. They
want me to quit, she told herself. That's why Gary
does rotten things to me while Lisa and the others
ignore me. They want me out and Samantha in.

She didn't know how she knew this but it felt right, and it brought about a change of mind – a fierce determination. No, she thought, turning off the shower and rubbing herself with a scratchy towel, they're not going to force me out if that's their little game, because I won't go. I'll hang on. I won't even mention this rotten trick to Mr Hepworth or Mrs Evans. I won't tell Mum either. I'll say it was an accident. I slipped and fell down the banking. Mum'll know a way to save my dress. Next rehearsal, Gary Bazzard and his friends are going to find me there as if nothing's happened. And the one after that, and the one after that – right up to the great day itself. And if they don't like it, they can go take a running jump.

While Fliss was undergoing her change of mind in the shower, Gary, Trot, Lisa and Ellie-May were stowing the dismantled worm in the Year Eight stockroom. Their mood was subdued as they awaited the consequence of their leader's vicious act. 'You're an idiot, Gary,' said Ellie-May. 'I bet she's in with old Hepworth right now, laying it on. We'll all be out, you see if we're not.'

Gary shrugged. 'She asked for it, and anyway, I couldn't help it. Something came over me.'

Lisa shot him a venomous glance. 'Something came over you? We're gonna lose the best kick any of us ever had, and all you can say is something came over you?'

'I don't think she'll tell,' said Trot.

Gary sneered. 'You're joking.'

'No I'm not. I know Fliss Morgan. She's got a stubborn streak. You and Lisa have been making it pretty obvious we don't want her around. I reckon she'll stick, just to spite us.'

Ellie-May sighed. 'I hope you're right, Trot. I want to do the park again like last night. It was the most fantastic feeling I've ever had.'

'Well that's what I mean!' cried Gary. 'That feeling. It comes over you and you can't help what you do. It's – awesome.'

'Yeah!' Trot smiled dreamily. 'Maybe next time we'll run into somebody – somebody we can scare.'

'If there *is* a next time,' muttered Lisa.

The four spent the afternoon in a state of suspense, but nothing happened. Fliss avoided their glances in class and kept well away from them at break, but nobody was summoned to the Deputy Head's office and Mrs Evans gave no sign she was aware of anything amiss. The only sticky moment came at home-time, when Mrs Evans found Lisa carrying part of the worm through the girls' cloakroom.

'Where are you going with that, Lisa?'

'Taking it home, Miss.'

'What on earth for?'

Lisa's brain raced. 'Er – safety, Miss.'

'Safety? What d'you mean, safety?'

'Schools get broken into, Miss. We wouldn't want vandals smashing up our worm.'

'I see. So you intend carting the whole thing backwards and forwards every time there's a rehearsal?'

'Yes, Miss.'

'Hmmm. Well, rather you than me, Lisa, that's all I can say. Off you go.' She went out on to the step and watched for a moment as Lisa joined Gary and the other two in the yard and the four of them went off up the driveway with their burdens. She and the Deputy Head had undertaken not to interfere in the play – it was to be an independent Year Eight effort, and if the children had decided to keep some of their props at home, so be it. Lisa's reasoning seemed decidedly odd, but then a lot of the things children do seem odd to adults, and Mrs Evans supposed there could be no harm in what they were doing.

Which just goes to show how wrong you can be.

# CHAPTER TWENTY-FOUR

Hughie Ackroyd hated kids. Until his retirement four years earlier he'd been a crossing keeper on the railway, and it seemed to him that he'd spent half his life chasing kids off the line and the other half making them stay off. The only thing he'd liked about his job was the bit of garden which went with the keeper's cottage. He'd kept that garden so beautiful that travellers in passing trains used to go 'Ooh!' and 'Aah!' as they whizzed by, and some of them would look back with their faces pressed against the window till Hughie's crossing was out of sight.

Now that he was a pensioner, old Hughie didn't have the garden any more. He and his wife lived in an old folks' bungalow. The grass outside was mown by the council, which also sent young men to tend the flowerbeds. Bored out of his skull, Hughie had taken an allotment on a nearby block and started growing his own vegetables. He'd turned out to be as good with vegetables as he used to be with flowers, and his leeks sometimes won prizes at local shows, which made him happy.

What didn't make him happy was this. One of the plots on the block was derelict. It had been derelict for many years and had become a jungle of couch-grass, weeds and brambles. This abandoned plot happened to be right next to Hughie's immaculate one, and in one corner of it stood a dilapidated greenhouse. This greenhouse had an old iron stove inside, and a bunch of kids sometimes showed up on wet weekends to light this stove and mess around in the greenhouse. They weren't doing any harm, except that occasionally, when there was nobody about, they'd pop on to somebody's plot and help themselves to the odd raspberry or handful of currants. They were trespassing though, and anyway Hughie hated kids. If they turned up when he was on his plot he'd shout over the rickety fence which separated his garden from the jungle, shaking whatever implement he happened to be holding, telling them they were trespassing and threatening them with the police. They'd gaze at him sullenly for a while then slink off through the rain, calling him rude names under their breath. This had been going on for at least two years, and the hatred he felt for them was matched by their dislike of him.

One of these kids was Gary Bazzard. Another was David Trotter. The rest were friends who attended a different school and went round with Gary and Trot at weekends and in the holidays.

Old Hughie's miserable face floated into Trot's mind that Wednesday evening when he, Gary, Lisa and Ellie-May were hanging around Trot's garden gate. Three weeks ago the girls wouldn't have been seen dead with the boys outside school hours, but lately the four had found themselves drawn to one another by an attraction each avoided thinking about, though they knew it had something to do with the worm. Mrs Trotter, watching them through her front window, told herself that if her son had started taking an interest in girls it was probably that Gary's fault, and decided to mention it to her husband.

'What we gonna do?' said Ellie-May.

Gary grinned. 'What d'you think?'

'The park, of course.' This from Lisa.

'No.' Trot shook his head. 'I've got a better idea.'

They all looked at him. 'What?'

'Old Ackroyd.'

Lisa frowned. 'Who's he?'

Trot explained. 'He practically lives on that allotment. He'll be there till it's too dark to see his stupid lettuces or whatever.'

'So?' Ellie-May looked quizzical.

'So we take the worm over to the allotments, get into it and spook the living daylights out of him. What d'you reckon?'

'I dunno.' Lisa pulled a face. 'He's old, you said. He might have a heart attack or something.'

'Will he heck! If he'd a bad heart, he wouldn't be able to dig that massive allotment, would he?'

Gary shook his head. 'He'd be at home all the time, watching telly and popping pills. I say let's do it.'

So they did.

# CHAPTER TWENTY-FIVE

'Yes, Sir?' The young constable looked across the counter at the elderly man in grubby overalls. He couldn't see the man's boots, but he could see the muddy tracks they'd left on the gleaming lino tiles and they irritated him. There's a doormat, he felt like saying, so why don't you use it? He wanted to say that, but instead he said, 'Yes, Sir?'

Hughie Ackroyd glared. 'I want to report an act of vandalism.'

'What sort of vandalism, Sir?'

'Mindless vandalism, of course. The sort you get because bobbies don't walk the streets any more.'

'And where did this – vandalism occur, Sir? Were you a witness?'

'Of course I was a witness. It was my allotment, wasn't it?'

'I don't know, Sir.' The constable reached out, slid a thick notepad towards himself and fished in his pocket for a ballpoint. 'I think we'd better start at the beginning. Can I have your name, Sir?'

'Hugh Ackroyd.'

The constable wrote on the pad. 'Address?'

The man sighed. 'Twenty-two, Alma Terrace. Look – do we have to go through all this? By the time you've finished fossicking about, that dragon'll have vanished without trace.'

The constable looked up. 'Dragon, Sir?'

'That's what I said.'

'You want to report an act of vandalism by a dragon?'

'Yes. Well – it wasn't a real dragon, of course. It was kids dressed up.'

'Kids dressed up.' The policeman put down his pen. 'How many kids were there, Sir?'

'I dunno, do I? They were in this dragon thing. I were packing up for the night – hoeing my last row of spring onions – and this contraption comes running through the gate. It – they – trampled all over my beds, pushed my incinerator over and ran off laughing.'

'I see. At about what time was this, Sir?'

'What's that got to do with it?'

'It's procedure, Sir.'

'It's a waste of flippin' time, that's what it is. I might have known there'd be no point coming here. You're all too busy cruising about in your luxury limousines these days, talking into them poncey radios, so why don't you just forget it, eh? Pretend I never came in. I'll take care of this – my way.' He spun on one mud-caked heel and made for the door.

'I wouldn't advise—' The constable broke off as Hughie Ackroyd slammed out. 'Watch out for those dragons, Sir,' he murmured to the still-quivering door.

# CHAPTER TWENTY-SIX

As Hughie Ackroyd was tracking mud into the police station, Trot was doing the same to the kitchen at home. His mother shrieked as he clomped across the floor. 'Look at the state of your shoes, David. Take them off at once and leave them on the mat.'

Trot turned with a sigh. 'Yes, Mum.'

'Wherever have you been to get them in that state?'

'Oh – around. You know.' Squatting by the doormat, fiddling with his laces. 'The park, mostly.'

'You must have been on the flowerbeds to get so filthy.'

'Maybe. We didn't mean to.'

'No. Anyway, your dad and I would like a word with you.'

'A word?' Trot's heart lurched. 'What about?' Surely old Ackroyd hasn't been here, he thought. He couldn't possibly know it was me.

'About you,' said his mother unhelpfully. 'Your dad's in the front room.'

Trot left his trainers on the mat and trailed after his mother. His father smiled up at him from an easy chair. 'Hello, son.'

Oh-oh. Trot returned the smile. Something's up. 'Hi, Dad.'

'Sit down a minute, David.' His father indicated the other chair. Trot sank into it, watching his parents' faces. They didn't look mad or anything. His mother sat down on the sofa.

'So, how're things going, son?'

Trot pulled a face. 'OK, I guess.' He couldn't remember the last time his father had asked him how things were going. There probably hadn't been a last time, so what was all this about?

'Good, good. The play?'

'Fine.'

'Your friend – Gary, is it?'

'He's fine too, Dad.'

'Good. I expect he's got a girlfriend, eh – good-looking lad like him.'

The way his father chuckled as he said this switched on a little light in Trot's head. Ah, he

98

thought. So that's what all this is about. Girlfriends.

'Er – no.' He shook his head. 'Not that I know of.'

'Oh.' His father shrugged. 'It's just that your mother and I seem to have seen quite a lot of Lisa Watmough and the Sunderland girl just lately, and we wondered —'

'They're in the worm, Dad. We have to practise, y'know?'

'Oh yes, of course. So you're not particularly interested in either of them, then?'

Trot shook his head. 'No way. Ellie-May's a droop and that Lisa's got a face like the back end of a motorway pile-up.'

'David!' his mother frowned. 'That's not very nice, is it?'

'What – Lisa's phizog?'

'No – you know perfectly well what I mean. Talking like that. Lisa Watmough's quite a pretty girl. I was at school with her mother and she was pretty too.'

'Good.' He looked from parent to parent. 'Is that it, then? Can we have the telly on now?'

His father looked at him. 'Thirteen's a difficult age, son. You know you can always talk to me and your mum if anything's worrying you, don't you?'

'Sure I do, Dad. Nothing's worrying me, honestly.' Quite the reverse, he thought, recalling the expression on old Ackroyd's face as he watched the worm mess up his stupid garden. Everything's fine. And it's going to get a whole lot finer.

'Good.' His father gripped the arms of his chair and levered himself upright. 'There's a film on Channel Four you might enjoy. I think I'll stroll down to the club for half an hour.'

When her husband had left the room, Mrs Trotter looked across at her son. 'Are you absolutely sure you're not fretting about anything, David?'

Trot grinned. 'Absolutely, Mum. There's nothing I can't handle. Nothing in the world.' As he said this, something occurred to him which wiped the grin off his face and caused his heart to kick. How is it, he wondered, that I saw the look on Ackroyd's face when only Gary has eye-holes?

# CHAPTER TWENTY-SEVEN

Fliss's mum left the dress to soak over Wednesday night in a strong detergent, and when she lifted it out of the bowl next morning and held it up to the light, the stains seemed to have gone. 'We shan't know for certain till it's dry,' she cautioned, but Fliss smiled tightly and said, 'It'll be fine.'

Lisa wasn't anywhere in sight when she got to the end of the road, but when she was halfway to school she heard someone call her name. She turned. Vicky Holmes was hurrying to catch her up. 'Hi, Fliss,' she smiled, falling into step. 'I – I just wanted to say I think it's rotten what they did to you yesterday. That lovely dress.'

Fliss nodded. 'Thanks, Vicky. My mum washed it. It's going to be OK.'

'Yes, but still.'

'I know. Gary Bazzard's a pain. He's always been a pain, but he seems to have got a lot worse since we've been doing this play. The others have too. I think they're trying to get rid of me.'

'Rid of you – how d'you mean?' Vicky looked horrified.

Fliss grinned. 'I don't mean murder, Vicky. I mean they want me out of the play.'

'Why?'

'Dunno. I don't think they know either.'

Vicky looked at her. 'That's a funny thing to say.'

'Yes I know, but it's true. It's like something's gotten hold of them since they've had that costume. Look at Lisa Watmough – she was my best friend.'

Vicky nodded. 'I've noticed.' She laid a hand on Fliss's arm. 'I'm your friend, Fliss.'

Fliss smiled. 'I know, and I'm glad. I mean it.'

That afternoon there was a long rehearsal in the double-games period. Everybody was in costume except Fliss, who felt a wally in skirt and jumper, waving her plastic sword. She was apprehensive too but she didn't let it show, and when Gary reached for her she hissed, 'You dump me down that bank again and I swear I'll smash your stupid costume once and for all. You wouldn't like that, would you?' No reply came from inside the worm, but when Gary's fingers touched her sleeve the creature shrank back in a most convincing way.

'Begone, foul fiend!' cried Fliss, pointing her sword towards an imaginary fen. 'I command you – in God's name begone, and come this way no more.' Very quietly, through lips which scarcely moved she added, 'You don't get rid of me that easily, Bazzard.'

The monster slunk away.

# CHAPTER TWENTY-EIGHT

Saturday morning, Fliss left the house at eight forty-five. It was day one of the Festival, and walking home together Friday afternoon she and Vicky had arranged to meet in Butterfield's diner to drink Coke and watch the procession with which the Festival was to open. Somebody at school had suggested putting the worm in the procession but Gary had dismissed the idea. He said it would spoil the surprise.

Elsworth was a small town and Butterfield's was its only supermarket. The diner which was tacked on its side was a favourite meeting place for kids. As she turned on to the road which dropped down into town, Fliss was thinking about the bridesmaid dress. Dry and ironed, it bore an indistinct mark where the edge of the stain had been, but this mark was so faint you'd have to know it was there before you'd see it. It certainly wasn't going to stop her wearing it for the play next weekend, so Gary Bazzard's dirty trick didn't matter any more. And, she told herself, since I've found a brand-new friend, Lisa Watmough doesn't matter either.

It was five past nine when Fliss reached Butterfield's, and Vicky was already there. She'd bagged a table by the window so they could watch the parade in luxury and pull faces at any boys who might go by. She had a can already, so Fliss got a Coke from the cabinet and paid at the counter before sliding in beside her.

'Hi, Vicky. Been here long?'

Vicky shook her head. 'Three, four minutes. Grant Cooper and Michael Tostevin just went by. They've gone to McDonald's.'

'How d'you know?'

'They mouthed it through the window. Probably hoped we'd join them.'

'No chance.'

'What'll we do after the procession?'

Fliss shrugged. 'Whatever you like, as long as it doesn't involve Grant and Michael. I see enough of them at school.'

They lingered over their drinks, turning and giggling when a knot of older boys looked in the window.

One of them was tall and lean, with thick black hair and a cheeky grin, and Fliss wished he'd come in and whisk her away to somewhere romantic, but he only stretched his mouth with his forefingers till it looked like a letterbox and wiggled his tongue at them. As he was doing this, the Mayor's limousine came cruising by at the head of the procession and the boy moved away, looking abashed. The girls' vantage point turned out not to be so great after all, because their view was partly blocked as shoppers lined the pavement to watch the floats. As soon as the last float had passed, Fliss and Vicky slurped up the dregs of their Cokes and went outside.

They strolled through the town. The spectators were dispersing, leaving crisp packets and bits of torn streamer on the ground. When they came to where the Odeon used to be, there was just a gap with bits of smashed masonry and the marks of heavy tyres. They stood for a while gazing at the gap, and Fliss told Vicky about the demolition man and the fabric he'd given to Lisa and herself.

They walked on, through the shopping centre and into the square. The parish church – St Ceridwen's – overlooked the square, and as the girls approached they saw that somebody had stuck a colourful poster on the notice board. They stopped to read it.

## ONE THOUSAND YEARS IN ELSWORTH

it began. 'What a thought,' groaned Fliss. 'One Saturday morning's bad enough.'

'Yes, but look,' cried Vicky. 'It mentions our play.'

'Where?'

The poster listed a whole lot of things which would happen during the coming week. Fliss's eyes slid down the list. There was the procession they'd just watched, with a prize for the best float; a Festival Queen, whom they'd glimpsed enthroned on the back of a lorry; a knockout quiz competition; a prize for the most original shop window display, and much else besides. At the foot of the list, in brilliant green, was this:

SATURDAY MAY 1ST. ON THE FESTIVAL FIELD. A THRILLING RE-ENACTMENT BY CHILDREN OF BOTTOMTOP MIDDLE SCHOOL OF SAINT CERIDWEN'S OWN STORY. SEE THE LEGENDARY CONFRONTATION BETWEEN THE DREADED ELSWORTH WORM AND THE FRAIL MAIDEN. SEE TERRIFIED VILLAGERS AND MARAUDING DANES. SEE CERIDWEN MARTYRED FOR HER FAITH. OUR TOWN HAS SEEN NOTHING LIKE THIS IN A THOUSAND YEARS.

'Bit over the top, isn't it?' said Fliss. 'People'll be expecting a Hollywood epic and all they'll get is us, trolling about like wallies in a bunch of home-made costumes.'

Vicky chuckled. 'Doesn't matter, Fliss. They'll love it anyway. They always do when kids're performing. It's like the infants' nativity play where someone forgets her lines or bursts out crying or goes wandering offstage looking for Mummy. The teacher's going ape-shape thinking the whole thing's ruined, but it isn't, because the mums and dads think it's really cute. They've seen the play fifty times before anyway, and it's the things that go wrong that make it interesting.'

'Hmm.' Fliss wasn't entirely convinced. 'We're not infants, Vicky. You heard what Mr Hepworth said. The whole town'll be watching us. It's the last thing, you see – the climax of the Festival. It's a big responsibility and it scares me.'

They moved on, strolling in a great circle round the town centre till they found themselves outside Butterfield's once more.

'Another Coke?' suggested Fliss.

Vicky shook her head. 'I'd better go. We're off somewhere in the car this aft – some garden centre or something, and I'll have to get changed. What you gonna do – find that lad you fancied?'

'Which lad?' Fliss looked indignant. 'I don't fancy

anyone. I thought I'd walk round the supermarket – get a choc bar or something.'

Vicky grinned. 'I'll believe you. Thousands wouldn't. You around tomorrow?'

Fliss shrugged. 'Dunno. Depends what the wrinklies're up to. I'll give you a ring.'

Vicky departed and Fliss went into Butterfield's. It was hot and busy and she knew she'd spend half her time being jostled and the other half dodging trolleys, but then nothing's much fun by yourself and it was too early to go home. If she'd known what was about to happen among those crowded aisles, she'd have gone home anyway.

# CHAPTER TWENTY-NINE

While Fliss and Vicky were reading the poster outside St Ceridwen's, Gary and the others were arguing in Trot's garage, which had become a sort of head-quarters for them. This was where they stowed the pieces of the worm, and where they usually met. It was a big garage with plenty of space to spare even when the Trotters' Astra was in it, as it was now.

'I still say let's frighten some people,' insisted Gary. 'We all know how great we felt after we did it to old Ackroyd.'

'Yes,' said Lisa, 'but that was at night, and in a quiet spot. Going downtown in broad daylight's another matter. We'd get arrested.'

'It was you got in trouble for being out late,'

countered Trot. 'So Saturday morning should be just the job, right?'

'Yes,' put in Ellie-May, 'but what about the police, Trot? Wouldn't we be disturbing the peace or something?'

'Would we heck! Listen – Gary and me aren't stupid. We've got it all worked out. You know the other week, when the bookshop did that promo on kids' books?'

Ellie-May looked at him. 'Yes – what about it?'

'Well – they had guys dressed up, didn't they? There was a bogeyman, a puppy and an owl, all walking up and down the street in front of the shop. Did they get arrested?'

'Well no, but they were advertising something, weren't they?'

'Exactly!' Trot smiled. 'And so are we. If anybody asks, we're advertising our play, right?'

Ellie-May shook her head. 'I'm not sure, Trot. I don't know if we'd get away with it.'

''Course we would. And anyway, nobody's going to ask. Come on.'

Fliss was making her way towards the checkout with a three-pack of Snickers in her basket. The narrow aisle was thronged with trolley-pushing shoppers and their children. Just in front of Fliss, a kneeling youth was taking tins of peas from a trolley and stacking them on a shelf. The trolley blocked off half of the gangway, creating a bottleneck into which impatient customers were funnelled, pushing and shoving one another in their eagerness to progress.

Fliss was being swept towards this bottleneck and wishing she'd gone home with Vicky, when she became aware of some sort of commotion between the checkout line and one of the exits. She couldn't see very well because the stacked goods on the shelves were higher than she was and because people were craning to see, but there seemed to be violent movement in the crowd over there and she could hear exclamations of anger or maybe surprise.

Seconds later, the forward momentum of the crowd she was in ceased. For a moment, Fliss and those about her stood absolutely still. Then somebody screamed and the surge went violently into reverse as those at the front recoiled from whatever it was they could see. Fliss back-pedalled desperately as a tidal wave of shoppers threatened to overwhelm her. To her left, an old lady cried out and toppled, clawing at a pyramid of cans in a useless bid to stay on her feet. The pyramid collapsed, pelting the woman with cans as she fell. Other shoppers, skidding and stumbling through scattered cans, abandoned their trolleys, which became rolling barriers against those who came after. A child fell and was snatched by its mother from the jaws of certain death.

Fliss turned and fought her way to the top of the aisle where she clung to a freezer-cabinet. Bodies cannoned into her, threatening to sweep her away, but she hung on, and as she clung there, limpet-like, she saw the worm. It was coming along the walkway between the tops of the aisles and the fixtures which lined the back wall of the store. It was moving quite rapidly for a thing its size, scattering shoppers as it came. It passed within a metre of her, heading for the last, wide aisle which would lead it back to the end of the checkout line. Fliss watched as it swung round the bend, dragging its iridescent green tail, and disappeared from view. Then she turned with a moan and threw up over a hill of turkey parts.

# CHAPTER THIRTY

Stan Morris had the biggest milk round in Elsworth. Seven days a week he was up at four-thirty and out delivering by five, and he'd work till ten at night, loading up his float for the next day. He followed this punishing routine the year round except for two weeks each January when he took Mrs Morris off to Florida. Renowned throughout the town for his addiction to hard work (some called him a workaholic), Stan would never win any prizes for the size of his imagination. In all of his forty-six years he had never seen a ghost or a UFO or a fairy and he never expected to, and he felt only scorn for those who claimed they had. So when a dragon crossed the road in front of the float at five-fifteen that Sunday morning, it came as a bit of a shock. He braked hard, causing the stack of crates on the flatbed to hit the back of his cab, and sat staring at the gap in the fence through which the apparition had vanished.

Mebbe the wife's right, he told himself. P'raps I have been working too hard. When a man starts seeing things it's time to slow down a bit.

Stan recovered his composure after a few minutes and drove on, and by eight o'clock he'd convinced himself he'd seen nothing unusual. Not that morning, nor any other morning of his life. For Stan, the unusual was deeply suspect and probably didn't exist.

Trot closed the garage door as silently as possible and tiptoed into the house. It was still only six o'clock. As far as he could tell, nobody had stirred. He crept upstairs and into the room he shared with his eight-year-old brother. As he eased the door closed, Jonathan rolled over in his bed and mumbled, 'Hnnn – where you been, David?'

'Sssh!' Trot pressed a finger to his lips. 'Mum and Dad are still sleeping, kiddo. It's early. I went to the bathroom, that's all.'

'Hmmm. OK.' The child rolled over again, pulled the duvet up around his ears and went back to sleep. Trot sat down on his own bed and bent forward to unfasten the laces of his Nikes, grinning as he did so.

Brilliant. It was brilliant. I'd give a million quid to see that wassock's face when he looks out the window.

The wassock Trot referred to was Percy Waterhouse, the Park Keeper, who was forever chasing teenagers, including Gary and himself, away from the kids' playground. Most teenagers still have a bit of the kid in them and they like the occasional swing or go on the roundabout and there was no harm in it that Trot could see, but Percy didn't agree. Big lugs, he called them, shouting and shaking his stick. 'Gerrawayfromthereyabiglugs!' What was a lug anyway, and who'd call their kid Percy, for crying out loud?

Anyway. Trot kicked off his trainers and stretched out on the bed with his hands behind his head, smiling at the ceiling. We paid him out this time, that's for sure. I wish I could be there when he sees what's left of his tulips. He'll go ape-shape. Cry in his cornflakes. He'll call the police but they'll not catch us.

A little voice in Trot's head told him that what they'd done was wrong, but that only served to broaden his grin. Wrong? Of course it was wrong. That was the whole point. He and his friends were discovering that doing wrong was fun. Oh, there was fear – a nagging, niggling fear behind the euphoria, which had little to do with the police and everything to do with the fact that, inside the worm, the four of

116

them became one, in ways which Trot preferred not to think about. They saw through Gary's eyes, didn't they? Danced to his tune, submerged their minds in his, but so what? The kick was awesome, and afterwards they were their old selves again, so that was all right, wasn't it?

Well, wasn't it?

# CHAPTER THIRTY-ONE

Ellie-May Sunderland's sister was away at college, so there was nobody to wake and ask her where she'd been when she slipped into her room. The Sunderlands always slept late on Sundays, so once she had her door closed she was safe. She should have been able to sleep, but for some reason she couldn't. She got undressed and slid in between the sheets, but then she just lay there thinking. She thought about how excited it made her feel to get into the worm with the others – how wonderful to be part of that invincible team. She remembered yesterday in Butterfield's – how people scattered at their approach. Their cries. The expressions of fear and disbelief on their faces. A part of her – some part she paid no attention to because she didn't want to – kept asking how you could see the expressions on people's faces when you're the end bit of a worm. Deep, deep down, she knew that something was happening to the four of them. Something awful. Trouble was, the excitement was so intense she didn't want it to stop, and so she tried not to think about it. Instead, she thought about the Park Keeper's tulips.

Terrific tulips they were. White and yellow, purple and scarlet, all round the Park Keeper's house – a rippling sea of colour with the house in the middle like a galleon. Every spring they were there, and people would make a detour in their journeys across the park to look at them. Ellie-May could remember when she was very young, being taken by her mother to see the flowers. How tall they'd seemed on their long stems – half as tall as Ellie-May herself. Nobody grew tulips like Percy Waterhouse, and he was proud of them.

Not now though. Not this year. It's amazing what eight busy trainers can do to a bed of tulips in the space of a couple of minutes. When Ellie-May closed her eyes she could see what they'd done. She could see the blooms lying bruised and broken on the trampled earth, their lovely petals crushed and stained with soil. She could see the torn leaves, the snapped-off stems tilted drunkenly one against another like the masts of a wrecked armada. She could see all of this

119

when she closed her eyes, as though the backs of her eyelids were a screen on which a video played, and it didn't make her feel good. She'd felt good while they were doing it. Then, her excitement had been intense, exhilarating. She'd laughed and whooped as she stomped and trampled, laying waste in seconds what had taken months to create. It had imparted a sense of power, a feeling that ancient wrongs were being avenged.

But now she only felt sad. Sad and frightened. What she and the others had done was wrong. She knew that now. Wrong, and stupid. Turning beauty into ugliness. Joy into tears. Good into evil. She thought of resigning her part – of giving up her place in the worm – but even as she thought about it, she knew she wouldn't. It was too wonderful, that buzz – that overwhelming wave of excitement, that sense of power. For some reason Ronnie Millhouse came tottering into her mind. Ronnie the drunk, who couldn't give up the thing which was destroying him. I'm hooked, she thought, just like Ronnie. The notion appalled her, but there it was.

'We do the most awful things,' she murmured aloud. 'Roll on the next time.'

# CHAPTER THIRTY-TWO

'Well – what d'you reckon?' Percy Waterhouse looked at the Detective Constable. It was ten o'clock Sunday morning and the two men were standing among the Park Keeper's vandalized flowerbeds. 'It was obviously kids – it always is, but which kids? Have they left any clues?'

The policeman shook his head. 'That's what I'd have said, Sir. Kids. In fact, I'd have bet on it, but it seems I'd have been wrong on this occasion.'

'What – you mean adults did this? But why, in heaven's name? It's so senseless.'

The detective shook his head again. 'It wasn't adults either, Sir, as far as I can tell. It appears to be the work of some sort of animal.'

'Animal?' cried Percy. 'That's absolutely imposs-ible. What animal would work its way systematically round a garden, breaking every single bloom? I don't believe it.'

'Well, Sir, I wouldn't have believed it myself, but there are no human footprints that I can find. Not one.'

'But you found animal prints?'

'Oh yes, Sir. Everywhere.'

'And what was it – a dog? A pack of dogs? What?'

'I don't know, Sir. Not yet. I'd like a veterinarian to look at them before making any comment.'

'Will you show me some of these prints? I think I can recognize dog prints without having to ask a vet.'

'Certainly, Sir. Look here.' The Detective Con-stable stooped and pushed some bruised stems aside with his palm.

Percy Waterhouse squatted and peered at the tram-pled soil. What he saw made him draw breath sharply. 'Good lord!' he gasped. 'What on earth made that?'

The policeman withdrew his hand and straightened up. 'What indeed, Sir. D'you see now why I'd like an expert opinion?'

'Yes I do. It's amazing.'

'Did your wife or yourself hear anything during the night, Sir?'

'No. Not a thing. I knew nothing about this till

I opened the bedroom curtains and saw the mess. I assumed it was a straight case of teenage vandalism and rang the police.'

'OK, Sir – I think that's all for now. I'm going to leave a uniformed officer here to see that the ground remains undisturbed till the veterinarian's had a look at it. Will you be at home most of the day, Sir?'

'Oh, yes. At home, or patrolling the park.'

'Then I'll be in touch. Goodbye, Sir.'

'Goodbye, Constable.'

Percy stood gazing at the ruins of his garden. As he did so, he became aware that he was not alone. He turned and found himself looking at the pathetic figure of Ronnie Millhouse. The drunk was standing at the edge of the public footpath, regarding the Park Keeper through red-rimmed, watery eyes. As Percy turned and saw him, he nodded his unkempt head at the smashed flowers. 'Shame.'

'Yes.' Percy felt a stab of irritation. What did the town drunk know about tulips? What could he possibly care? He was probably about to cadge fifty pence or something.

'I reckon that there dragon done it.'

Dragon? Percy frowned. What was the idiot on about? He glared at Ronnie. 'What are you talking about?'

Ronnie gazed earnestly at the Park Keeper, who had spoken sharply, but whom Ronnie knew to be

123

knew that Percy knew he used the
sleeping in, and that he could have
if he felt like it, but he didn't. Not
let him stay, but he sometimes left a
bit of g a plastic bag for him to find. He never
came when Ronnie was there, and if asked he'd have
denied feeding the drunk, but Ronnie knew. When
you're as alone as Ronnie, you develop a sharp nose
for a friend.

'The dragon,' he repeated. 'I seen 'im t'other night,
up the top path. Long he were, and green.'

Percy smiled faintly in spite of his grief. 'Not
pink, then, Ronnie?'

Ronnie shook his head. 'Green. I hid behind a
tree till he'd gone. I reckon it was 'im done this,
Mister.'

'Well.' The Keeper smiled again. 'It's as good a
theory as any I've heard up to now, Ronnie.' He
smelled bacon frying and turned towards the house.

The drunk called after him. 'I'm right, Mister,
you see if I'm not.'

Percy waved a hand without turning. 'Thanks,
Ronnie. I'll bear it in mind.' He went in to his
eggs and bacon, wondering briefly what Ronnie's
breakfast would be, and when. As for the poor chap's
dragon story, Percy had forgotten it before he closed
the door.

# CHAPTER THIRTY-THREE

Percy Waterhouse wasn't the only one calling the police that Sunday morning. Len Butterfield had spent a sleepless night wondering who it was who'd caused chaos in his supermarket the day before. He hadn't been there when it happened, but his manager had called him and he'd arrived before the staff had done much clearing up.

The scene which greeted him had made him very angry. The place looked as though a bomb had gone off inside it. Shelves were down. Cans and packets littered the aisles. Smashed bottles lay everywhere, their sticky, multicoloured contents spilled across the tiles. Abandoned trolleys stood with their tyres in this congealing goo. And worst of all, he'd found himself surrounded by a knot of irate customers who had been awaiting his arrival. Some of these customers had cuts and bruises to show him. Others displayed articles of their clothing torn, or decorated with globs of bleach, jam, mustard pickle and yeast extract. All of these people preferred their clothes the way they'd been before, and threatened to sue Len Butterfield for the cost of cleaning, repairing or replacing them. They seemed to think he was to blame for what had happened – they thought the monster or whatever it was had been some sort of publicity stunt gone wrong.

He tried to tell them it wasn't – that he knew nothing about it – but they were in no mood to listen. They'd all seen the weird collection of creatures outside the bookshop the other day. They knew traders would pull practically any sort of silly stunt to draw attention to their businesses, and it seemed obvious to them that Len Butterfield's stunt had simply got out of hand.

He'd smoothed it over in the end – made promises, given undertakings, and the customers had departed more or less satisfied. Some of them wouldn't be back though, and what with one thing and another, this stupid prank by persons unknown was set to cause Len a lot of unwanted hassle.

His manager had called the police and they'd arrived while Len was striving to soothe his customers.

They'd taken statements and poked about a bit, but they hadn't seemed all that interested and Len had suspected his little spot of bother wasn't serious enough for them. Nobody was dead or in hospital, nothing had been stolen, and any loss would probably be covered by insurance.

So at eight-thirty Sunday morning, after a restless night and with a pounding head, Len rang the station to demand a progress report. The sergeant at the other end was polite, but not helpful. Investigations had been made, and were continuing. There had been no significant developments so far, and if there were developments, Len would be informed. At this stage, said the sergeant, they were treating the matter as a prank, probably by children, which had got out of hand.

Which means, muttered Len, when he'd hung up and was making coffee, that you don't intend doing anything about it. You'll stick the statements in a file, shove the file in a drawer and forget about it. But I won't. I won't forget. I'll do my own investigating, and woe betide whoever did this when I get hold of them.

127

# CHAPTER THIRTY-FOUR

It wasn't until seven in the evening that the Detective Constable got back to Percy Waterhouse. During the afternoon the Keeper had seen a woman he'd assumed was the veterinarian, squatting among the remains of his tulips with some sort of measuring device, but he hadn't gone out. He was too depressed to feel like talking, and anyway she was working for the police and probably wouldn't have told him anything. He'd watched through the window till the woman finished whatever it was she was doing and left with the uniformed constable, and he'd almost given up hope of hearing anything that day when he answered a knock on the door and found the detective on the step.

'Evening, Sir. May I come in?'

'Of course.' Percy stepped back to admit him, then closed the door and showed him into the sitting-room. 'Have a seat. Coffee?'

'Oh, no thanks. I had one at the station.' He smiled apologetically. 'There isn't a lot I can tell you, actually.'

'What did the vet say?'

The policeman shrugged. 'Not a lot. Reckoned the prints were like nothing she'd seen. Said they might have been made by a very large reptile but were far more likely to be an elaborate hoax.'

'Hoax?' cried Percy. 'Why would anyone want to pull a hoax like that – and how would they do it?'

The detective shook his head. 'I've no idea, Sir. We checked to see whether any large reptiles have been reported missing. They haven't, though we're continuing to monitor that. And we've searched the park. Oh, and I think I should tell you that while we were doing that, Jimmy Lee came sniffing around.'

'Jimmy Lee?'

'Yes, you know – chap from the local rag. Reporter. Nose like a ferret and features to match. Anyway, we had to tell him something so we gave him the elaborate-hoax line.' He grimaced. 'No doubt there'll be a piece in the *Star* about it. Thought I'd warn you.'

'Yes, thanks. And you really believe it was a hoax?'

'It's the likeliest explanation, Sir. We don't get a lot of large reptiles in Elsworth and anyway, what sort of reptile would do this sort of damage to a garden? Though as I said, we're still checking for possible escapes.'

'Well.' The Keeper gazed glumly out of the window. 'All I can say is, if it was a hoax I hope you catch the hoaxer. Oh, and by the way, there's at least one chap who'd go along with the large reptile theory.'

'Who, Sir?'

Percy smiled. 'Ronnie Millhouse. Swears he saw a dragon in the park the other night.'

'Yes, well.' The detective smiled too. 'Ronnie's got a whole menagerie of creatures inside his head, and they're all pink.'

'Not this one. Green, he reckons. Sure you won't have that coffee?'

'No thanks.' The policeman stood up. 'I'd better be off, Sir. We'll keep you informed if there are developments.'

'Thanks.' They walked to the door and Percy let his visitor out.

'G'night, Sir.'

''Night, Constable.'

He stood for a while, staring morosely at what was left of his garden. Then he sighed deeply, turned, and went inside.

# CHAPTER THIRTY-FIVE

Jimmy Lee's scoop had broken too late for Monday's *Star*, so the people of Elsworth knew nothing of the dragon-and-tulip affair as the children of Bottomtop Middle streamed into school that Monday morning. Year Eight had planned no rehearsal for today – Mrs Evans had told them there was such a thing as being over-rehearsed – but in the event they had to sacrifice double English and get into their costumes because the vicar arrived during registration to ask how things were progressing.

They did it on the field, it went smoothly and the Reverend Toby East was impressed. When it was over – when Gemma Carlisle, the Viking Chief, had dragged Ceridwen off to her martyrdom between the goal-posts – he applauded. He actually stood there on the touchline with a smile on his face and clapped. Mrs Evans, who had stood beside him throughout the performance, clapped too. She felt she ought to, since Mr East had given the lead. He turned to her, beaming. 'Splendid!' he cried. 'Isn't it absolutely splendid, Mrs Evans?'

'Oh yes,' smiled the teacher, who would rather have been taking the double English lesson she'd prepared. 'Our Year Eight is a very able group, Mr East.' The children, who had heard the vicar's enthusiastic remark, came trooping across the field wearing bits of costume and smug grins. Even Fliss was smiling. Nothing unpleasant had happened and she was feeling better.

The vicar beamed at her. 'A fine Ceridwen, my dear – serene and lovely as the saint herself if I may say so.'

Fliss dropped her eyes, felt herself blush and murmured, 'Thank you.' She wished he hadn't singled her out for praise – Gary Bazzard wouldn't like it, and she was anxious that he should be propitiated till after Saturday.

The vicar said something to Mrs Evans, who nodded. He turned to the children. 'Would the four children who play the worm please remain here for a moment?'

Fliss saw that his smile had gone and felt a spasm of unease. Please don't stir them up, she thought. It's me that's got to face them on Saturday.

Mrs Evans touched her shoulder. 'Come along, Felicity.' The class was making its way back into school. Fliss followed, hoping the vicar had kept the four to praise them; knowing he had not.

'Now.' The vicar regarded the quartet sternly. 'I'm going to ask the four of you a question, and I want you to answer me truthfully. Is that understood?'

Gary Bazzard nodded. The others mumbled, 'Sir.'

'Where were you at ten past eleven last Saturday morning?'

'At my granny's,' said Gary at once. 'You can ask my mam.' The others looked at him and said nothing.

The vicar sighed. 'And you, young lady – where were you?'

Lisa looked from Gary to the vicar and back again, biting her lip. 'It's no use, Gary,' she said. 'He knows.'

'Yes.' The vicar's tone was icy. 'He knows, but he's waiting to hear it from you. Where were you?'

133

'Butterfield's,' mumbled Lisa.

'Supermarket,' said Ellie-May.

'In costume,' admitted Trot.

'Thank you,' said the vicar quietly. 'You might be interested to know that one of the shoppers in Butterfield's that morning was my wife. Your antic upset her quite badly, but unlike everybody else she knew about the play and realized where the monster must have come from.' He frowned. 'I suppose you know what a wicked thing it was that you did?' Nobody answered. 'You know, don't you, that your silly prank might have had disastrous consequences? Somebody frail – a weak heart perhaps, and they might have died. Did you think about that? Did you consider the possibility of somebody being trampled, crushed – somebody's baby? Did you think at all before you did what you did?'

Lisa sniffled. 'No, Sir.'

'No, Sir.'

The vicar gazed at them. 'Why did you do it, eh? Whatever possessed you to do such a thing?'

'Possessed?' Gary glanced sharply at the vicar. 'Nothing possessed us, Sir. It was a stunt. A publicity stunt, to advertise our play. We thought it was a good idea, Sir, that's all.'

The vicar looked at the boy. 'Your idea, was it?'

'Yes, Sir.'

'Well, it was not a good one, Gary. Far from it. People were injured. Frightened. Property was damaged. And there was nothing to connect the event in people's minds with your play. If, as you say, it was a publicity stunt, it was poorly thought out and brutally executed, and I'm ashamed of you. Your classmates have worked hard to produce an outstanding presentation, and the four of you have let them down with this act of – of vandalism. Do you know that the police are involved?'

'Police?' Trot looked scared.

'Of course.' The vicar sighed again. 'Oh, it's all right. You needn't worry. I'll go to them. Tell them it was a publicity stunt gone wrong. I'll talk to Mr Butterfield too. It will be all right. But I want you to promise me that you'll never ever do anything of the sort again. Do I have your promise?'

They nodded. 'Yes, Sir.'

'Good. Then we'll say no more about it. That's a very fine costume you've constructed. Most realistic. Keep on rehearsing, and good luck for Saturday.'

'Thank you, Sir.'

The vicar strode away, and the quartet walked slowly across the yard. 'What now?' asked Lisa. 'We've given our promise.'

'Our promise?' Gary kicked a stone. 'What're you – an infant? Our flipping promise!'

'He's the vicar, though. A promise to a vicar's sort of special, isn't it?'

'Oh, yes.' The boy grinned wolfishly. 'It's special all right. I'll get special pleasure out of breaking it, that's what's special about it.'

# CHAPTER THIRTY-SIX

Tuesday morning, seven-thirty. The Morgans at breakfast. Mrs Morgan sips coffee. Mr Morgan hides behind the *Star*. All you can see of him is his fingers and the top of his balding head. Fliss takes the last slice of toast from the rack and begins to butter it. Her knife makes a scratchy sound on the toast. The *Star* is lowered slightly. Her father glares at her over the top of it. He doesn't say anything. He doesn't need to. 'Sorry,' murmurs Fliss. She butters more quietly. The *Star* rises to its former position. Silence, which Mr Morgan breaks with a scornful laugh. His wife and daughter glance up, waiting to know what's funny. Without lowering the paper, Mr Morgan begins to read aloud. Fliss wonders how he knows they're listening.

'Park Keeper Percy Waterhouse called the police on Sunday morning when he found his formerly beautiful garden had been wrecked in the night. When the constabulary arrived at the scene, huge reptilian footpri··s were found all over the Keeper's tulip beds. A veterinarian who examined the prints dismissed them as a hoax, and a police spokesman told our reporter, "We don't get a lot of large reptiles in Elsworth." However, when our reporter spoke with Mr Ronnie Millhouse, a resident of the park, Mr Millhouse claimed to have seen a large dragon there only a few nights ago. Most people would doubtless be inclined to discount this evidence, but before doing so they ought perhaps to consider the following: Elsworth once played host to a very large reptile indeed. This reptile was no hoax – it ate people. The beast was never killed – it was simply banished to the fen. This was exactly one thousand years ago. This week the people of Elsworth are celebrating its banishment.

Prematurely—?'

Mr Morgan stops reading. The silence lasts several seconds.

'Go on,' says Mrs Morgan.

'That's it,' her husband tells her. 'There's no more.'

'What an odd story,' says Mrs Morgan.

'Damned silly if you ask me,' growls Mr Morgan. They both chuckle.

Fliss does not.

Because of the impromptu run-through for the vicar on Monday, Tuesday's rehearsal was cancelled. Fliss was glad. She couldn't get the *Star* story out of her head. Common sense told her that Gary and the others must have been on the rampage again, but would they dare do such a dreadful thing? And what about the prints? How had they managed those? She longed to ask Lisa but knew she mustn't. Lisa wouldn't tell her anyway. From time to time during that seemingly endless day she watched Lisa and the other three, hoping they'd give themselves away by some word or expression but, though the dragon story was the chief topic of playground conversation, she detected nothing which might indicate their guilt in the affair. She discussed it at lunchtime with Vicky, who said it couldn't have been them – the footprints would have been far too difficult to fake.

Nevertheless, Fliss worried. She worried all day at school, and all evening, moping around at home. Finally, at nine o'clock, she could stand it no longer. She should have been thinking about going to bed, but she knew she wouldn't sleep till she knew what had happened Saturday night in the park. Her parents exchanged glances when their daughter announced that she fancied a pizza takeaway and got into her jacket, but the takeaway was only round the corner. 'Don't be long, dear,' was all her mother said, and her father chipped in with, 'And don't talk to any strange men.'

She reached Trot's gateway and hesitated. Suppose Trot and the others weren't here? She knew they met most evenings, but maybe not tonight. Well, she told herself, if they're not here I'll knock on the door and ask to see Trot. I'll tackle him head on – ask him straight out whether he and the others wrecked the Keeper's flowers, and how they made the prints. It might even be easier if he's by himself. I'll swear not to tell on them, if only he'll set my mind at rest. Yes. That's what I'll do. I sort of hope he is alone. She took a deep breath and strode up the path.

They weren't there. The garage door was up, but the place was empty. There was no car. And when she crept inside and looked around, there was no worm either. The costume had gone.

She tried the house. There were lights on inside, but nobody answered her knock. With

140

the car gone, it was likely the Trotters were out for the evening. And with the worm gone, it was likely the foursome were out for the evening too.

Where? As she turned and hurried down the path, Fliss felt a tingling in the nape of her neck. She half ran along the road, glancing back from time to time to make sure nothing was following her. She was so scared she almost forgot to get her pizza, and when she got it home she couldn't eat it. She shot it into the pedal-bin and ran upstairs to her room. Her parents exchanged glances again.

'Hormones,' said Mrs Morgan.

'Aaah,' said Mr Morgan.

# CHAPTER THIRTY-SEVEN

If there was one thing Jimmy Lee enjoyed more than sniffing out a good story, it was his pigeons. They were racing pigeons and Jimmy had twenty of them, not counting squabs. He kept them in a loft he'd built himself, on an allotment opposite his house. This allotment was on the same block as Hughie Ackroyd's, and the two men were on nodding terms. Hughie didn't care for pigeons and Jimmy wasn't interested in growing vegetables, but they did have one thing in common – they were both worried about the kids who hung around the abandoned greenhouse. Bored kids often got up to mischief, and a neat garden or a well-ordered pigeon loft might well act as magnets to acts of casual vandalism.

So when Jimmy looked out of his window that Wednesday morning and saw that the door of the loft was swinging in the breeze, his first thought was that his birds had had a visit from those flipping kids. Fearful for the welfare of the squabs, he pulled on some clothes and hurried across the road, to find that the situation was very much worse than he had feared.

The first thing he noticed was the smell. It was a pungent smell and Jimmy recognized it. It was the smell of burnt feathers, and he could smell it before he reached the loft. He hurried forward, cursing under his breath, and cried out in horror and disbelief at the sight which met his eyes.

They'd had the place on fire. The structure itself hadn't burned, but the inside walls were scorched as though somebody had stood in the doorway and discharged a flame-thrower. Dead birds littered the floor, their plumage blasted off. Charred feed-bags spilled their contents among the corpses, and inside the nest-boxes his precious squabs lay roasted on beds of blackened straw. So intense had been the heat from whatever it was the vandals had used, that the loft's window had cracked across two of its four panes. A quick count told Jimmy that not all of his birds had died, but of the survivors there was no trace.

He was trudging back, intent on calling the police, when he saw the footprint. There was only one, in

143

a patch of soft earth near the gate. Jimmy squatted, tracing its outline with a finger. It was big – maybe thirty centimetres across, and it had been made by something heavy because the depression was at least four centimetres deep. In fact, it was exactly like the prints the police had shown him in the park yesterday.

'Some hoax,' he muttered, straightening up, wiping soil from his finger on his jeans. 'Some rotten hoax.' Tears of grief and rage pricked his eyes. He kicked a stone viciously with the toe of his trainer and strode towards the house.

# CHAPTER THIRTY-EIGHT

'Mr Bazzard?'

'Yes.'

'We're police officers. You have a son, I believe – Gary, isn't it?'

'That's right. Why – what's he done?'

'I haven't said he's done anything, Sir. We'd like a word though. Is he in?'

'Yes. Upstairs. You'd better come in.'

It was six o'clock Wednesday evening. Gary's mother was out. She worked the evening shift at the biscuit factory. Her husband was glad. She'd have a fit if she was here, he told himself. Police asking after our Gary. He went to the foot of the stairs.

'Gary!'

145

'What?'

'Someone to see you.'

'Who?'

'Police.' The loud music which had been issuing from his son's room ceased abruptly and Gary peered over the bannister.

'Police? For me? Why?'

One of the two officers looked up at him. 'Come on down, son, and we'll tell you.'

Gary descended like a man on his way to be hanged. His father led the officers into the front room. 'Sit down if you like. Do I stay or what?'

'Stay if you wish, Sir. This won't take long.' Both officers remained standing. They looked at Gary. 'You're at Bottomtop Middle, aren't you, son?'

Gary nodded warily. ''Sright.'

'And you're involved in a play. Part of the Festival.'

'Yes.'

'You're part of a dragon thing, aren't you?'

'The Elsworth Worm. I'm the head.'

'A remarkably realistic beast, by all accounts. Where is it?'

'Sorry?'

'Where is it – the prop, costume, whatever you call it?'

'Oh – it's at Trot's place. David Trotter's. He's part of it too.'

'You keep it at your friend's house?'

'Yes.'

'And what do you do – do you get into it sometimes and practise for the play?'

'We rehearse, yes.'

'Who's we, son? How many of you are there?'

'Four.'

'Names?'

'David Trotter. Ellie–May Sunderland. Lisa Watmough. And me.'

'And you rehearse together?'

'We have to. It's not easy, moving together and all that, when only one can see.'

'I can imagine. Where do you rehearse?'

'Trot's garden. The street. Anywhere, really.'

'Hughie Ackroyd's allotment, perhaps? Butterfield's supermarket?'

'I – we don't use anybody's allotment. We did go round the supermarket last Saturday, but that was for publicity.'

'Publicity?'

'For the play. It was sort of an advert.'

'Pretty violent advert, son.'

'I know. The vicar told us off. It like – got out of hand.'

'I'll say it did. And what about the stunt in the park, and the one with Jimmy Lee's pigeons? Did they get out of hand too?'

'I don't know what you mean. What stunt in the park? What pigeons? I don't know anything about any pigeons.'

'Tell me how you do the footprints, son.'

'Footprints?' Gary looked bewildered. 'I don't understand.' He appealed to his father. 'Dad – I don't know what he's on about.'

Mr Bazzard looked at the officer. 'What's this all about, Officer? Why are you questioning my son?'

The officer told him. When he'd finished, Mr Bazzard frowned. 'And you think my son'd do something like that? Destroy somebody's garden? Burn up a man's pigeons? He's just a kid, for Pete's sake.'

'We're not accusing him, Mr Bazzard. We're simply making enquiries.' He turned to Gary. 'David Trotter – you know his address?'

'Sure. Thirty-three Baslow Grove. He'll only say the same as me.'

'I want to take a look at this worm of yours, son. See what sort of feet it's got.'

'Our feet. It's got our feet, that's all.'

'Then you've nothing to worry about, have you, son?'

They left. Gary told his father about the supermarket and reaffirmed the quartet's innocence in the other matters the officer had mentioned. Then he went up to his room, turned up the volume on his CD player, and lay on his bed wondering who had set the police on to him, and in what way the blabbermouth might be made to pay. .

# CHAPTER THIRTY-NINE

'Are you feeling all right, Fliss?' Thursday morning. Fliss playing with her cornflakes, watched by her mother who looks concerned. No, Mother, I'm not feeling all right actually. I'm tired, and I'm scared. Fliss doesn't say this, though it's the truth. It would lead to questions she'd rather not try to answer. She wants only one thing. She wants Saturday to come and go so normal life can resume. Till then she wants to be left alone. She forces a smile.

'I'm OK, Mum.' I'm not though. I fret, I dream, I fret some more. Things are happening. Frightening things. Things there are no words for. And the ship sails on.

This is the ship. This house, the street outside,

150

people's lives. The good ship Elsworth, sailing towards disaster while everybody dances. The only one who knows is me and I'm just the cabin boy. If I tried to tell them, they'd laugh.

'You don't look too well, dear. Didn't you sleep?'

'A bit. It's just the play, Mum. I'll be fine when we've done it.'

'Hey, listen to this.' Dad, from behind his paper. How do I know it's Dad, thinks Fliss. It could be anyone with thin hair and thick fingers. Someone different every day.

'What is it, dear?' her mother enquires.

Dad grunts. 'Another dragon story, but not so joky this time. Listen.' He reads out the piece Jimmy Lee has written. The one about his pigeons, and how a hoax can go too far. Fliss puts down her spoon and gazes into her bowl. Her fingers pluck at a corner of the tablecloth, pleating, smoothing, pleating. Nobody notices. Dad comes to the last bit – the bit where Jimmy says that somewhere in Elsworth there's a dangerous person – perhaps even a madman – and that the sooner he's caught the better. He stops reading and lowers the paper. His wife sighs, shakes her head and murmurs, 'Some people.' Fliss stops playing with the tablecloth and picks up her spoon. Her hand trembles and she feels sick. All she can think is, Tuesday night. It happened Tuesday night and they were out. I know, because I went round and there was nobody there. It was them, and on Saturday I've got to face them. Or it.

On Saturday, I'm the pigeon.

# CHAPTER FORTY

Mrs Watmough shook her head and clucked into her coffee. Her husband had gone to catch his London train and she was lingering over a second cup, the *Star* spread before her on the table.

'What is it, Mum?' Lisa, clearing breakfast things, leaned over her mother's shoulder.

'This.' The woman tapped an item with a fingernail and Lisa read the headline. PRIZE BIRDS BLASTED IN LOFT RAID.

'Where was this?' she asked. 'What happened?'

Her mother read out the piece, then shook her head as before. 'There's some wicked folks about,' she sighed. 'They want locking up, or worse.'

Lisa picked up the toast rack and butter dish. 'It's awful,' she said. 'Poor little things.' She turned away to hide her shining eyes, remembering the reek of burning feathers.

# CHAPTER FORTY-ONE

Fliss set off as though going to school, but she didn't go. She'd remembered something her dad had read out on Tuesday about Ronnie Millhouse. Ronnie had claimed he'd seen a dragon in the park. What did he mean? Did he mean a real dragon, or people dressed up? Was he drunk when he saw it? People said Ronnie Millhouse was permanently drunk. Well, OK, but did that mean he wouldn't be able to tell a real dragon from a pretend one? There was only one way to find out.

She was desperate. If she hadn't been, she wouldn't have dreamt of approaching Ronnie Millhouse. She was afraid of him. All the kids were, because of the shouting. Most of the time, Ronnie was quiet, but now and then he'd go off his head and start shouting. Spit would fly from his lips on these occasions. He'd wave his arms about and shake his fists and the things he shouted made no sense. When he was like that, even adults gave him a wide berth.

She knew where he'd be at this time of day. He'd be at the bus station, cadging change from people going to work. And if he'd already left there, he'd be by the stall in the market where he went to buy a mug of tea and get warm.

He wasn't in the bus station, so Fliss hurried across to the market and found him by the tea stall with his big raw hands wrapped round a steaming mug. The stall owner was wiping off his counter but there were no other customers. Probably there wouldn't be till poor Ronnie moved on.

Fliss approached gingerly, praying that the drunk wouldn't start shouting. She didn't want people to see her talking to him. She was ashamed of herself for feeling like that but she couldn't help it. She drew near, smiling.

'Hello.'

'Hello, love. No school today?'

Relief washed over her. He sounded just like anybody else. She shook her head. 'I'm not well.' Which is true enough, she thought.

'Poor lass. Cuppa tea, is it?' For a moment she thought he was offering to buy her one, but when he made no move towards the counter she realized he wasn't, and was glad.

'No. I – I saw your name in the paper.'

'Oh aye? What'd it say then?'

'It said you saw a dragon in the park.'

'Dragon?' Ronnie's eyes clouded over and his face creased up with the effort of remembering. 'Oh, aye. The dragon.' He smiled ruefully. 'Nobody believed me.'

'I do.'

'Do you?' He grinned at her. 'Good for you. It's hard when you tell the gospel truth and nobody believes you.'

'I know.' She smiled. 'It happens to kids all the time. What was it like?'

'What was what like?'

'Your dragon, Mr Millhouse.'

''Twern't my dragon, love. I only saw it, that's all.'

'Yes, but what was it like? Was it kids dressed up?'

'What?' He glared. 'I thought you said you believed me?'

'Oh, I do!' She said this quickly, afraid he'd start shouting. 'I'd like to know what he looked like, that's all.'

'Well, he weren't nobody dressed up, I can tell you that. He were long and green and his head was up in the air. Red eyes, he had, and fire in his mouth.'

'Fire? Are you sure?'

''Course I'm sure. He passed me as close as you are now, and I felt the ground shudder from his footsteps. Scared I was, I can tell you.'

'And had you ever seen him before?'

Ronnie shook his shaggy head. 'No. Never before, never since, nor never want to neither.'

'Oh.' She'd learned nothing that was of comfort, and didn't know how to break off the conversation. She looked at her watch. 'I must get on.'

'Doctor's, is it?'

'What?'

'Doctor's – you being unwell and all?'

'Oh – yes, that's right. Ten past nine at the surgery. 'Bye, Mr Millhouse.'

'Mind how you go, love – there's some funny people about.' He glared about him at the early shoppers. 'I SAY, THERE'S SOME FUNNY PEOPLE ABOUT!'

Fliss turned and fled.

# CHAPTER FORTY-TWO

It's impossible, surely? A real dragon. The actual Elsworth Worm. Ronnie Millhouse is a drunk, right? And drunks see things that aren't there – pink elephants and stuff.

So why did I go and see him? I wish I hadn't. A bunch of kids dressed up – even violent kids who hate you – is one thing. I can handle that. But the actual worm—

Ah, come on! What are you, Fliss Morgan – two years old? An infant, scared of the Big Bad Wolf?

There wasn't much point going to school till lunchtime, so to avoid being seen truanting she'd come to the park. People walk through parks, of course – especially on warm spring mornings like this one

– so Fliss had found a nice quiet spot where she could sit and think. The old bandstand stood in a forest of laurel and rhododendron gone wild, in a part of the park which was seldom visited except by kids at weekends and young couples in the evening. It was Ronnie Millhouse's bedroom, of course, but Fliss didn't know that. She thought the pile of old newspapers and bin liners under the bench must have been dumped there by some wally too idle to find a litter bin.

She was scared now. Really scared. The more she thought about recent events, the more convinced she became that something sinister was happening. All right, there might not be an actual worm – probably never had been; it was just a legend – but something had definitely happened to Lisa and the others. They'd changed. Before, they were just ordinary kids. Sure, they got up to mischief now and then like anybody else, but they'd never have dreamt of invading Butterfield's or trashing somebody's garden. And as for that awful thing with the pigeons— She shook her head. It wasn't them. It couldn't have been. Fire had been used. They'd never do that. They'd changed, but not that much.

And yet— She was thinking about last Saturday in Butterfield's. It was a bit hazy now – she'd sort of blotted it out – but what exactly had she seen? What had all those shoppers seen to make them panic as they did? Some kids dressed up? A papier-mâché head and eight trainers pounding the floor? Try as she might, Fliss couldn't remember those eight trainers. She thought she remembered something else. She thought she could remember four sturdy legs and gigantic birds' feet slapping the tiles. Birds' feet with long, crescent talons— But no – she must be mistaken. It must have been an hallucination – a shared hallucination. They happen. Hundreds of soldiers once thought they saw an angel hovering over the battlefield at a place called Mons. And the Indian rope trick – that was supposed to depend on spectators sharing the same hallucination.

It wasn't a convincing explanation. It didn't make her feel any better. A draught kept stirring the papers under the bench, making them rustle. Making her jump. It was a quiet spot she'd chosen. Too quiet. After a while she decided she'd rather risk being seen by somebody who knew her than remain in the bandstand. She got up and walked out into the sunshine, which failed to cheer her.

# CHAPTER FORTY-THREE

Fliss approached the school gate at ten to one, and the first person she saw was Lisa. She dropped her eyes and made to pass her former friend without speaking, but Lisa said, 'We didn't expect to see you again till Monday. We thought you'd got the message.'

Fliss stopped. 'What message?'

Lisa sighed. 'The message we've been sending you for weeks now. Stay away. Don't play Ceridwen. Fall sick. Let Samantha do it instead. That's what understudies are for.'

Fliss gazed at her. 'I don't get it. What difference is it going to make whether I play the part, or Samantha? The ending'll be the same.'

'No it won't. If you play the part, something

terrible will happen to you. If you don't, it will happen to Samantha. That's the difference.'

'What is this terrible thing you say will happen, Lisa?'

Lisa sighed again. 'Have you heard about Jimmy Lee's pigeons?'

Fliss swallowed hard. 'Yes, I've heard. What about it?'

'We did that.'

'What? I don't believe you. You wouldn't burn little baby birds in their nests.'

'We wouldn't, but we did. And we wrecked Percy Waterhouse's tulips, and we got away with it too.' Lisa's eyes gleamed. 'The police came to Trot's. Searched.' She laughed. 'They wouldn't tell us what they were looking for, but we knew. They were looking for some gadget they thought we had for making footprints. They didn't find anything, of course, and Gary said, "Even if we did have a way of making prints, there'd still be our own footprints, wouldn't there? How would we get rid of them, Officer?" Lisa laughed again. 'Officer, he called him, in this very sarcastic voice.'

Fliss looked at her. 'And what's the answer, Lisa? How do you do it?'

Lisa's grin faded. She shivered. 'You wouldn't believe me if I told you,' she said. 'I can hardly believe it myself.'

163

'Try me.'

'No. Listen, for the last time. Something's started here which nobody can stop. I tried to tell you right at the beginning, remember? I said it was as if something was taking over, making things happen. Well, I was right, and now this thing's in control and none of us could stop even if we wanted to. You'd have to be inside the worm to understand, but you're outside and you're in the way, and that's not a smart place to be. We've been friends, Fliss, and that's why I'm warning you. Stand aside, or suffer the consequences. I can't make it any plainer than that.'

Fliss gazed at her. 'I don't believe you, Lisa. I don't understand some of what's happened but I think it's you and Gary and Trot and Ellie-May, playing some sort of game. You've done some cruel, stupid things to try to frighten me, but I don't believe you burned the pigeons. Somebody else did that, and you're just using it to make yourselves seem ruthless. I'm going to be there on Saturday, and that's where your game will have to stop because there's nothing special about the four of you, Lisa. Nothing. You're a bunch of kids, that's all, and once the play's over they'll scrap the costumes and that'll be that.' She spun on her heel and strode off down the driveway.

Lisa gazed after her. 'You're wrong, Fliss,' she murmured. 'You've no idea what you're up against, but you'll find out. Trouble is, by then it'll be too late.'

## CHAPTER FORTY-FOUR

Friday afternoon had been set aside for a last full-dress rehearsal on the school field. They hadn't rehearsed Thursday afternoon, but the whole of Year Eight had gone with Mr Hepworth across town to get a look at the Festival Field. Sarah-Jane had taken notes and made sketches, so that everybody would know where to stand and how to move during the actual performance.

Lunchtime. For Year Eight this meant a quick bite, then off to the changing-rooms. They'd done it all before and things had generally gone well, but everybody was feeling nervous just the same. This was it. The final run-through. Next time they took the field, it would be the real thing.

Fliss hung back a bit when it was time to change. She wasn't in the early part of the play anyway, and she didn't particularly want to run into Lisa and Ellie-May. All they had to do was put on green tights – they'd get into the worm on the banking behind the goal-posts – so they shouldn't be long in the changing-room. She loitered in the yard till she saw them leave, then went in.

She'd hung the bridesmaid dress on a peg that morning so that any creases might drop out. As she approached it, she saw that somebody had fastened a small sheet of paper to the bodice with a pin. With hands that shook she pulled out the pin and smoothed the paper. It had been torn from a jotter, and somebody had scrawled a verse on it in pencil:

NEVER WORRY
SLEEP ALL DAY
NEVER GO TO SCHOOL
NEVER TIDY UP YOUR BEDROOM –
BEING DEAD IS COOL

She read it through twice. Whoever had written it had used block capitals so there was no handwriting to identify him, but Fliss knew who the poet was. She balled up the paper and flung it into a corner. 'Never give up, do you, Gary Bazzard?' she murmured. 'But you might as well, because here comes the bridesmaid.'

The rehearsal went perfectly. Mrs Evans and Mr Hepworth watched from the touchline as the worm terrorized the villagers. This was Year Eight's favourite bit, and it went on for some time. It never got boring though – the worm was wonderful to watch, and each of its victims had a different way of screaming. They watched as the beast came strutting from its fen to claim another life and found Ceridwen standing in its path. They thrilled in spite of themselves as the creature lunged, roaring, at its frail adversary, but they knew nothing of Fliss's relief when it brushed her dress, grew docile and slunk away.

The rest was easy. Gemma led her Vikings in a series of convincingly bloody raids on the village. More screaming. Having subjugated the villagers, Gemma demanded that they worship Viking gods. Ceridwen refused and was butchered. There was a brutal-looking axe and plenty of tomato ketchup, but no screaming. Year Eight had decided that saints don't scream.

If they'd been anywhere near Fliss at two o'clock Saturday morning, they'd have learned how wrong they were.

# CHAPTER FORTY-FIVE

She awoke to utter darkness and a rank odour she could not at once identify. She was cold, and her bed seemed to have grown hard while she slept so that her back, bottom and heels felt bruised. Groaning softly, she tried to roll on to her side, but her right knee encountered an obstruction which prevented it bending. Puzzled, she flexed it again and felt the kneecap press against something which did not yield.

Unease stirred in her. She lifted an arm, and the hand struck something solid no more than a few centimetres above her face. A whimper constricted her throat. She groped frantically with both hands in the blackness, and the nails and knuckles scraped something smooth and hard. She tried to fling her

168

arms wide, but her hands thudded into solid matter, producing a hollow sound and causing pain. As this pain ebbed, she recognized the smell which filled the darkness. It was the reek of wet earth.

She could hear voices. Children's voices, chanting in unison:

NEVER WORRY
SLEEP ALL DAY
NEVER GO TO SCHOOL
NEVER TIDY UP YOUR BEDROOM –
BEING DEAD IS COOL

and it was then that she knew she was in her grave.

Screaming, she shot bolt upright and nothing stopped her. The mattress gave under her hands and bottom, and the reek of earth faded. There were footfalls and a flood of glorious light and then she was clinging to her mother, sobbing and shaking and babbling something about a grave. Her mother rocked her and stroked her hair, but it was some time before Fliss grew quiet.

# CHAPTER FORTY-SIX

Sunlight lay in dapples on her duvet when Fliss woke up. She knew she'd been dreaming, but could not remember her dream. It felt late. She rolled over, grabbed the clock on the bedside cabinet and gasped. Eleven. It was eleven o'clock. Practically everyone in Elsworth would be making their way to the Festival Field by now, ready for the afternoon's festivities. People would have been working since early morning, erecting stalls and stands, tents and booths. Hanging flags and bunting. Putting up signs and notices.

'Mum!' She sprang out of bed and began pulling on her clothes.

Her mother came hurrying up the stairs. 'Fliss

– are you all right, dear?'

Fliss nodded. 'Sure, but look at the time. Why didn't you wake me? You know we're doing the play today.'

'Of course I know, Fliss. It's at two o'clock. Your dad and I are ready, but there are three hours yet and we thought you ought to sleep on awhile after the dreadful night you had.'

'Did I have a dreadful night? I'm fine now.'

Her mother nodded. 'You certainly did, young woman. Two o'clock this morning, screaming your head off. You'd had a nightmare. Something involving a grave, from what I could make out. Don't you remember?'

'No. Well – vaguely. I was in my grave, I think, and somebody was singing.'

'You frightened me half to death, I know that. There's nothing worse than being woken in the middle of the night by a scream.'

'Sorry, Mum. I think I know what brought it on.'

Her mother nodded grimly. 'So do I, dear. It's this play. It's been worrying you for weeks. It's been like having a little stranger in the house, the way you've mooned and fretted. Not like you at all.'

Fliss nodded. 'I know.' And I'm still worried, she thought. More than worried. I'm scared. Not of Gary Bazzard and the others, though. No. Something else. Something'll happen today. Something that isn't in the script. I know it. I can feel it deep down, but I can't talk to you about it, Mum. Or Dad. You'd think I was barmy. No, it's something I've got to face by myself. Aloud, she said, 'Is my dress ready?'

Her mother nodded. 'I ironed it. Nobody'll notice the stain. Dad's put it on a hanger in the car.'

'Good. I mustn't forget my sword.' A plastic sword, she thought. What use will that be when it comes – whatever it is?

She tried to eat breakfast, but could manage only orange juice.

'You can't fight a dragon on that,' joked Dad. Fliss forced a smile.

And so it was that at a quarter to twelve on that sunny April Saturday, Fliss set out with her parents to face whatever it was that awaited her on Elsworth's Festival Field.

# CHAPTER FORTY-SEVEN

Trot had been up and about since six. He'd woken at five-thirty, full to bursting with energy and anticipation. Unable to suppress this he'd slipped out of bed, dressed silently and let himself out of the house.

He spent nearly an hour tinkering with the worm. He tapped extra staples into the frame at points where wire and wood threatened to part company. He used superglue to fix a couple of loose teeth. He gave the fabric a vigorous brushing where it had picked up splashes of mud, and touched up the paintwork here and there on the head. He whistled as he worked, because he felt that today was going to turn out special for himself and his three friends. Today they'd leave something behind and

173

start something new and nothing would ever be the same again.

At eight o'clock, Gary phoned. Was he ready? Was everything set? He sounded high, and told Trot that he'd phone Lisa and Ellie-May to make sure they were ready.

Ready for what? As he put down the phone, Trot felt a surge of dull fear. What was happening to them all? What was it they'd got into? How would it end? There were no answers to these questions. The fear was a part of the excitement – the sick kick he felt – and all Trot knew for certain was that the sensation was mounting and that he couldn't stop now if he tried.

It's going to be terrible, he moaned. The worst thing that anybody ever did. I don't know how we can even think of it.

Roll on two o'clock.

# CHAPTER FORTY-EIGHT

At twenty to two, Fliss slipped away from her parents with the bridesmaid dress folded over her arm and the sword concealed inside it. The field, outside the roped-off central arena, was thronged with people, and she had to dodge and weave her way through them as she headed for the marquee in which she and the others would change. There were still a few picnickers, but most people had packed away lunch and were watching two clowns wobbling on unicycles around the oval of cropped grass which formed the arena, juggling burning torches. The marquee stood at one end of the arena and when Fliss reached it, most of the kids were there already.

'Here's our Ceridwen,' grinned Mr Hepworth as she ducked inside.

Mrs Evans smiled tightly. 'Just in time, Felicity. Hurry up and change now.'

The marquee was crowded with Vikings and villagers. Fliss glanced around till she spotted Gary and the others, but they were occupied with their costume and didn't glance her way. She swallowed hard, told herself not to be silly, and began to change.

She'd put on the dress and was buckling her white sandals when the vicar arrived. He said something to Mr Hepworth, who clapped his hands to get everybody's attention. 'Listen,' he said. Andrew Roberts continued practising his narrative on Barry Tune. The Deputy Head glared at him. 'When you're quite ready, Andrew Roberts.'

'Oops – sorry, Sir.'

Mr Hepworth sighed. 'The Reverend East has a few words to say to you all, so pay attention.'

The vicar beamed. 'Good afternoon, everybody. In a minute or two I shall go to the podium to announce the commencement of your splendid production, but I thought I'd drop by here just to say how much I appreciate all the hard work you people have put in in the three weeks since Easter, and to tell you how much I'm looking forward to your performance.' He smiled. 'Good luck, everyone.'

'Thank you, Sir,' chorused Year Eight, high on

176

adrenaline. The vicar walked out into the sunshine.

Mrs Evans cleared her throat. 'Right, Year Eight, this is it – your big moment. You've worked terrifically hard and everything's fine, so don't worry. Go out there and enjoy yourselves, and the whole town will enjoy you too.' She smiled. 'Stand by, villagers. Ready, Ceridwen? Worm?'

There was a crackling noise through the public-address system as the vicar stepped up to the mike. 'Mr Mayor. Lady Mayoress. Ladies, gentlemen and children.' His voice echoed tinnily over the field. 'What a perfect day we are having to round off a truly memorable week.' He paused, smiling as a rumble of assent came from the crowd. 'We've been blessed with fine weather, not only today but all week. Each of our various events has gone splendidly and here we are, bathed in glorious sunshine and having the time of our lives.' More assent from his listeners.

'Let us not forget though, the reason for all this festivity. Let us remember whose heroism, whose martyrdom we celebrate here today.' A respectful silence settled over the field as Toby East spoke of how, exactly one thousand years ago, the village of Elsworth had been delivered from evil by the valour of its own dear saint, the maid Ceridwen, and of how this brave lass had later died a cruel death rather than renounce her faith. 'To remind us of these events,' he cried, 'and to bring to a climax this week of celebration, the children of Year Eight at Bottomtop Middle School now present their own production, entitled *Ceridwen – Heroine-Saint of Elsworth.*'

The vicar, with a sweeping gesture, indicated the marquee. There was a ripple of applause as Andrew Roberts emerged, followed by the villagers with Ceridwen in their midst. Andrew mounted the podium as the vicar vacated it. The villagers continued to the far end of the arena where a cluster of stalls and booths became the ancient village.

The narrator approached the mike. He was carrying his script, but in fact he was practically word-perfect without it. Vikings peeped from within the marquee as Andrew's voice rang out.

# CHAPTER FORTY-NINE

' "The time – a little over one thousand years ago. The place – Elsworth, then a mere village, set in the midst of misty fenland. Elsworth, a once quiet village where terror now reigns, for the nearby fen has become the dwelling-place of a monster – a monster known to every terrified inhabitant as the Worm." '

An area behind the marquee was the fen. As Andrew paused in his narrative, the worm came capering round the side of the marquee and entered the arena. Gasps of admiration and surprise came from the crowd, but these became boos and hisses as the spectators entered into the spirit of the event. At the far end of the arena villagers cried out, pointing and scrambling to hide behind stalls and one another as the

179

monster advanced. Fliss, who was not to appear till the worm had taken four victims, watched anxiously from behind a booth.

Everything went according to script. Gary's arms shot out and seized Tara Matejak, who screamed and writhed lustily as she was half carried, half dragged across the arena and away behind the marquee to the boos, whistles and catcalls of the crowd.

Michael Tostevin was the second victim. He threw away his mattock and tried to run, but the worm easily overcame him and he was borne away, howling, to join Tara.

When Haley Denton was seized, she managed to squeeze the contents of a sachet of ketchup all over her throat and chest. Cries of disgust and revulsion rose above the booing as she was dragged off, gurgling realistically and oozing gore.

Joanne O'Connor was to be victim number four. Fliss watched tensely as the girl moved on to the arena wielding a hoe, pretending to till the soil. Up to now everything was normal and Fliss felt a flicker of hope. She recalled what she'd said to Lisa on Thursday. '—that's where your game will have to stop because there's nothing special about the four of you—' At the time she hadn't been nearly as sure as she'd sounded, but now she dared to hope that she'd been right.

Joanne was working her way along a row of

imaginary carrots with her hoe. The worm was taking an unusually long time to appear and Fliss could see that Joanne was nervous. The poor girl didn't dare look towards the marquee because she wasn't supposed to see the worm approaching, but she was biting her lower lip and Fliss knew she just wanted her part to be over.

Fliss slitted her eyes against the glare of the sun and peered towards the marquee. As she did so, she heard a shrill scream and a figure appeared, running. It was Haley Denton, and she was followed by Tara Matejak and Michael Tostevin. Michael was trailing smoke and, as he pelted into the open, Fliss saw a flicker of flame and realized his tunic was on fire.

There were cries from people in the crowd. A woman ducked under the rope and sprinted towards the boy. She was carrying a car blanket. As Fliss watched, paralysed with shock, the woman brought Michael down with a rugby tackle and rolled him in the blanket. A man ran out to help her, but he'd got less than halfway when the marquee whooshed into flame and the worm came out of the smoke with fire in its jaws. The man cried out, skidded to a halt and ran back, scattering hysterical Vikings. The shrieking crowd milled as the monster blasted to left and right with jets of searing flame.

Andrew Roberts flung away his script, dived off the podium and vanished into the crush. Joanne

181

O'Connor abandoned her hoe and ran screeching towards where she thought she'd last seen her mother. An Army sergeant from the local recruiting office shouted to his five men to get into the armoured personnel carrier they'd been demonstrating. There was no live ammunition, but he thought that if they could ram the creature they might maim it. It was a bit of good thinking – one of the few bits to emerge in what was otherwise a shocked and panicky rabble – but it was to no avail. The first soldier was still some metres short of the A.P.C. when it was seized by two terrified civilians, who drove it off at speed.

The worm had advanced and stood now in the centre of the arena, snorting and clawing the turf with the talons of a gigantic bird. Its mad red eyes rolled this way and that and came to rest on the woman whose prompt action had saved the burning boy. She had flung her body across Michael's to prevent him rising. Now, as the monster swung its gaping maw her way, she cringed beside the heaving mound of blanket, helpless to save herself.

# CHAPTER FIFTY

All of this had taken place in the space of a few seconds, during which Fliss, transfixed with horror, had seen all of her worst fears realized. Even as her brain was telling her such things were impossible, she knew that the Elsworth Worm had returned. Her four classmates, together with the contraption they had made, had undergone an incredible change to become the nightmare beast which now possessed the field. The beast which had burned the pigeon squabs and trampled the tulips. The beast which had rampaged through the supermarket a week ago, creating panic. The beast which was about to annihilate the woman who now crouched helpless in its path.

She didn't think. She was incapable of thought.

But as the worm prepared to blast its victim, she ran on to the field, waving her pathetic sword and shouting to attract the beast's attention.

The worm swung its great head, watching Fliss through hate-filled eyes. A long, low growl came out of its throat. Through the corner of her eye, Fliss saw her father leap the rope, heard him scream her name. She dashed on. It was as though some force had assumed control of her mind, of her actions. She felt no fear now.

With a shattering roar, the worm launched itself to meet her, discharging a shaft of flame which passed so close she felt its searing heat. As they met in midfield she swung the sword at the creature's scaly neck, but it glanced off as though the beast were clad in steel. The monster dwarfed her as it reared to rip with its claws. She ducked and dodged as razor talons flailed the air. The flimsy sword windmilled around her head till, inevitably, it struck a horny claw and was torn from her grip.

It's over now, she thought. It must be. One slash of those talons and I'll fall in shreds. And even as she thought this, a voice in her head was crying, 'Forward. Only forward.' She pressed on without knowing why, ducking and weaving. So close was she now to her adversary that the worm could neither see her nor bring its fire to bear, and every time it backed up to get her range, Fliss moved with it.

It couldn't continue, and Fliss knew it. She felt herself tiring. Dimly, she was aware that the Festival Field was emptying as townspeople scrambled over walls and fences or fought their way through gateways. Perhaps, she thought, some will escape if they flee, but the worm will have its revenge on Elsworth, and slake its thousand-year hunger with Elsworth's dead. She wished her parents would save themselves, but knew they were near for her sake. Her limbs felt leaden and she couldn't get her breath. She knew that soon she must fall.

It happened almost at once. The worm backed up and, as Fliss followed, her sandal came down on a stone. She stumbled and fell, and before she could roll or rise, she was pinned to the turf by a great taloned foot. She gritted her teeth and screwed up her eyes, awaiting the blast which would finish her.

It didn't come. Instead, the worm emitted a chilling screech and the foot was snatched back. Fliss rolled and looked up. There stood the beast, but as she watched, its image began to shimmer and warp like an object underwater. She screwed up her eyes and shook her head. It was changing, shrinking. The coils of smoke, the jets of flame, became wisps and tongues which flickered out and dispersed before her eyes. The scaly armour seemed to soften and hang in folds and wrinkles, and the creature's sinewy limbs disintegrated, becoming thin and pale as the talons in which they ended curled and shrivelled like feathers in a flame. The screeching roar dwindled through cough, bark and groan till it resolved in the anguished cries of children.

A wave of nausea swept through Fliss and she closed her eyes. When she looked again the worm had gone. On the scorched and trampled grass lay a smashed thing – a contraption of wood and cloth and wire in the midst of which sprawled four ashen-faced children. A hand plucked at the sleeve of her dress. Fliss turned. The woman she'd saved gazed into her eyes. 'What – what was it?' she croaked. 'What happened?'

Fliss shook her head. She felt unutterably tired. 'I don't know,' she murmured. 'But whatever it was, I think it's over now.'

# CHAPTER FIFTY-ONE

A week went by before life in Elsworth returned to something like normal. During that time, two explanations emerged for what had taken place on the Festival Field.

The vicar said that Elsworth had once more been threatened, and once more delivered.

The *Star* abandoned its earlier sensationalism and said that the townspeople had been the victims of a collective hallucination, and of mass hysteria.

The town's churchgoers tended to favour the vicar's version, while the police and most other people went along with the *Star*. No prosecutions followed the recent spate of vandalism. Nobody felt like delving any deeper into the matter for fear of uncovering fresh mysteries. No. It was over and done with, whatever it was. Forget it. Life goes on.

Fliss could not forget it, and neither could Lisa, Ellie-May, Gary or Trot. They'd survived, but their horrific experience had left them feeling isolated – set apart somehow from the world of friends, family and everyday life. Saturday found them huddled in the greenhouse on the abandoned allotment. The spell of fine weather had broken down. Rain hissed and rattled on the grimy panes, there was no sign of Hughie Ackroyd, and they were glad of the warmth which came from the rusty stove.

They'd sat for some time in silence, letting a chill which had little to do with the weather thaw from their bones, when Lisa said, 'I don't know how you can stand to be with us, Fliss, after what we did to you.'

Fliss shook her head. 'It wasn't you, Lisa. It wasn't any of you. You were possessed – taken over by something. It started as soon as you were chosen to play the worm. It had waited a thousand years and it didn't rush. It took over your minds, little by little. Then it started changing your bodies, though you didn't know it. On Festival Day, behind that marquee, it extinguished you altogether and became itself once more –

the Elsworth Worm, bent on revenge. If others had been chosen, the same would have happened to them.'

'I know.' Ellie-May shivered. 'I could feel it. It was like – you know – you get an urge to do something you know's wrong, but the thought of it's so exciting you can't stop yourself. It was terrific and horrible, both at the same time.'

'I felt like that,' nodded Trot. 'I wanted to do the worst things I could think of, even though they were stupid and cruel. I just couldn't help it.'

'I knew something was happening,' murmured Gary. 'Deep down I knew, but I didn't want to admit it to myself. I was enjoying it all, you see. The power. People's fear. The destruction.'

'What I want to know,' said Fliss, 'is what it felt like when you actually became the worm. I mean, did you know you'd changed?'

Lisa shook her head. 'There was this terrific excitement, that's all. You felt like you could do anything. Anything at all. Everybody was scared of you, see? It gave you power – a feeling of power.'

'And hate,' put in Gary. 'You hated everybody and everything. You just wanted to smash everything in sight.' He grinned ruefully, shaking his head. 'You should've felt the hate we felt for you, Fliss. You and your plastic sword. It was awesome.'

'I felt it,' said Fliss.

'But you came on,' said Lisa, 'I wonder what would have happened if you hadn't?'

'We'd have become murderers,' said Trot. 'The four of us. We just wanted to destroy everyone and everything in Elsworth. We must've been totally crazy.'

Fliss shook her head. 'I told you, Trot – it wasn't you.'

'But if it hadn't been for you, Fliss, the worm would've won and we wouldn't exist as separate people – or as people at all, come to that.'

Fliss shook her head again. She smiled, her first smile in a long time.

'It wasn't me either,' she said.

## ABOUT THE AUTHOR

**Robert Swindells** left school at fifteen and worked as a copyholder on a local newspaper. At seventeen he joined the RAF for three years, two of which he served in Germany. He then worked as a clerk, an engineer and a printer before training and working as a teacher. He is now a full-time writer and lives on the Yorkshire moors.

He has written many books for young readers, including many for the Transworld children's lists, his first of which, *Room 13* won the 1990 Children's Book Award, whilst his latest, *Abomination*, won the 1999 Stockport Children's Book Award and the Sheffield Children's Book Award and was shortlisted for the Whitbread Prize, the Lancashire Children's Book Award *and* the 1999 Children's Book Award. His books for older readers include *Stone Cold*, which won the 1994 Carnegie Medal, as well as the award-winning *Brother in the Land*. As well as writing, Robert Swindells enjoys keeping fit, travelling and reading.

# ABOMINATION
## *by Robert Swindells*

Martha is twelve - and very different from other kids, because of her parents. Strict members of a religious group - the Brethren - their rules dominate Martha's life. And one rule is the most important of all: she must never ever invite anyone home. If she does, their shameful secret - Abomination - could be revealed. But as Martha makes her first real friend in Scott, a new boy at school, she begins to wonder. Is she doing the right thing by helping to keep Abomination a secret? And just how far will her parents go to prevent the truth from being known?

SHORTLISTED FOR THE WHITBREAD AWARD
WINNER OF THE SHEFFIELD CHILDREN'S BOOK AWARD

'A taut and thrilling novel from a master of the unpredictable'
*Daily Telegraph*

ISBN: 978 0 552 55588 3

# IN THE NICK OF TIME
### by Robert Swindells

'What year is this?'

When Charlie falls off a stepping stone in the woods, her whole world suddenly changes. She stumbles in the 21st century, and picks herself up in the middle of the 20th. There are no trainers, no mobile phones – and she's a pupil at a weird outdoor school where the classrooms don't even have walls.

Somehow, Charlie has slipped through a nick of time. Can new friend Jack help her find a way back – or will she be trapped in the past?

Inspired by a fascinating piece of British history, this is a gripping page-turner from multi-award-winning author, Robert Swindells.

ISBN: 978 0 552 55585 2

# NIGHTMARE STAIRS
## by Robert Swindells

*I'm falling - falling down steep, narrow stairs - if I hit the bottom asleep, I know I'll never wake.*

Every night Kirsty wakes up screaming. Every night she has the same terrible nightmare - of falling downstairs. But does she fall? Or is she pushed?

Then Kirsty discovers that her grandma died falling downstairs and she begins to wonder: is the dream hinting at a dark secret in her family? She has to know the truth. But tracking a murderer is a dangerous game, and as she delves into the past, Kirsty uncovers a secret more terrible than anything she can imagine.

A terrifying read from one of today's master storytellers.

WINNER OF THE SHEFFIELD CHILDREN'S BOOK AWARD
FOR BEST SHORTER NOVEL

'Cleverly put together - funny as well as gripping'
*Sunday Times*

ISBN: 978 0 552 55590 6